Lord Randal's Tiger

Elizabeth Chater

FAWCETT COVENTRY • NEW YORK

LORD RANDAL'S TIGER

Published by Fawcett Coventry Books, a unit of CBS
Publications, the Consumer Publishing Division of CBS Inc.

ISBN: 0-449-50182-5

Printed in the United States of America

First Fawcett Coventry printing: May 1981

10 9 8 7 6 5 4 3 2 1

To KEN FAIT

"Tiger! Tiger!"

Chapter One

LORD RANDAL BERESFORD was in a vile temper. This condition would not have been apparent to many members of Milord's acquaintance outside of his mother and his old nurse, both of whom had known him from a child and could therefore read even the faintest of signs: the slight rigidity of his handsomely flared nostrils, the imperceptible narrowing of the eyelids over his dark eyes, the faintest of white lines around his well-cut mouth. Since neither of these ladies, nor his best friend, Sir Peter Daley, was present at the Dog and Duck Inn at Smoulton, a wretched village with no claim to beauty or style, there was no one to mark his lordship's potentially explosive state in time to prevent disaster.

That his lordship's rage was directed in part toward himself did nothing to relieve the pressure. The previous evening, under the influence of a particularly potent brandy, Lord Randal had wagered a very large sum of money upon the outcome of a pugilistic encounter to be held just outside the aforesaid village of Smoulton. The other side of the wager had been taken by Sir Jerold Peke, a presumptuous demi-beau who should never have been admitted to the august salons of White's club. The fact that Peter Daley had taken his friend to task, not for betting with an encroaching mushroom, nor for the excessive amount of the wager, but for his stupidity in backing the challenger rather than the champion, had led to an acrimonious discussion with Daley in which a number of youthful quarrels had been referred to and refought.

As a consequence, Lord Randal went very late to bed, and what with the liquor and the heat of his quarrel, made a poor night. Forced to rise at dawn to drive to the boxing match with a severe headache, he snapped his groom's head off when that faithful retainer, bringing round his curricle, first announced that it was sure to rain, and then so far forgot himself as to inquire, increduously, if it was true that his lordship had been such a gapeseed as to back a sure loser in today's match.

At this point, Milord told Fenn where he could go, and drove off without him. Threading his way with practiced skill through the streets of London, Lord Randal mentally consigned to Perdition all long-time false friends, all servants who thought they had a license to criticize just because they had known one for donkey's years, all untrustworthy liquors, and all puffed up demi-beaux who thought themselves judges of the Fancy.

After a couple of hours in the fresh air, however, Milord, feeling slightly better, began to regret his hasty action in dispensing with Fenn's services. This regret was changed to anger when Lord Randal realized he had neglected to inform himself as to the correct route to

8

the obscure and probably unattractive village where the mill was to take place. Fenn would of course have known—it was his business to discover such routes—but Fenn was back in London.

At this point, Lord Randal drew rein in a small hamlet and asked directions of a Johnny Raw who further exacerbated Milord's temper by giving him confusing directions and, upon being challenged, saying that anybody but a knock-in-the-cradle would know how to find Smoulton, since there was a mill on that very day, and the road ahead was packed with every kind of carriage in the kingdom.

Looking beyond the narrow village street, Milord immediately discovered that the road into which it led was indeed packed with vehicles, all going one way. He was able to insinuate his own curricle into the line, not without some pretty ruthless jockeying, which earned him a stern reproof from a nattily-dressed gentleman, to which he paid absolutely no attention.

Flushed with this minor success, Lord Randal began to relax. True, his curricle was hopelessly locked into the press of vehicles, and the progress of the mass was annoyingly slow, but he was on the right road and would no doubt arrive in Smoulton in time to eat and freshen up at the inn and then, restored by a modest pick-me-up, proceed to a good seat at the boxing match.

At this moment, in a stunning demonstration of Fenn's prescience, the heavens opened and poured down a flood. A curricle offers no protection from the elements. Within minutes Lord Randal was completely drenched, soaked, and sodden. The press of vehicles crept forward with monstrous deliberation, a line of snails, worms, tortoises. Men inside carriages smiled pityingly. The rain continued to fall.

After an eon of crawling wretchedness, the cavalcade —or at least that section of it in which Milord's curricle was embedded—arrived at the miserable village of Smoulton. Naturally the place, which offered second-rate accommodation for fewer than one hundred, was jammed with several hundred Top-of-the-Trees sporting bloods, all of whom demanded first class lodging and food without delay. Lord Randal permitted himself a self-satisfied smirk at his own forethought in reserving a bedroom and meals in the better of the two inns Smoulton boasted. To his chagrin, he discovered that his room had not been kept for him, the scoundrelly landlord loudly protesting that he had never received the reservation.

"I am to suppose that someone has offered you a bribe," sneered Lord Randal. "I shall know better than to stay here again!"

The landlord, well aware that this descent of The Quality upon his mediocre hostelry was a once-in-a-lifetime opportunity, was not cast down by this threat, only inquiring with intolerable smugness whether his worship would wish to be accommodated in the attic room. "You'll have to share it with three other gentlemen, of course," he concluded briskly.

"I should not stay in this wretched hovel if you paid me," Milord was petulant enough to retort.

Since all his rooms were quadruply rented, and even his attics, barn, and stable were engaged, the landlord's withers were not wrung. "Then, sir, I wish you good luck," he said, grinning unforgivably.

Driving to the lesser of the village's two inns, jostled by freshly-arriving vehicles and young bloods on horseback, Lord Randal could imagine Fenn's comment on people who bit off their own noses to spite their faces, and was not soothed by the truth of the aphorism. In point of fact, he was, by the payment of an outrageous bribe, able to secure one half of a bed in a room which looked out onto a pigsty, with the reluctant

10

promise of a luncheon before and a dinner after the mill. With these doubtful blessings Milord was forced to be content. He knew none of the other guests who crowded the miserable hostelry, nor did he wish to do so. He even entertained the idea of pulling out for London immediately after the mill, but such was not to be. By the time the fight was over, twenty dragging rounds in an open field under continual downpour, Milord knew himself to be coming down with a racking cold, and even the crowded misery of a fetid room shared with strangers was preferable to a long drive through the rainy night. The meal, greasy meat and underdone vegetables, was climaxed by a doughy fruit pie which was completely inedible, some hard cheese, and an inferior port. Disgusted by the stout appetites and cheery demeanor of the sportsmen at his table, all of whom had backed the winner, Lord Randal retreated to a shadowy corner of the taproom, now full of other celebrating gentlemen who had chosen to place their blunt on the champion. Nursing his drink, his cold, and his chagrin over his own losing choice, Milord sipped at his wine as though it were vitriol, and regarded the festivities with a jaundiced eye.

There were two tables of cards already in play, and young men flushed with success and liquor were betting outrageously and noisily. After a time, Lord Randal rose and strolled over to watch the play at one table. In his present mood, the lack of skill of the gamesters pleased him; he watched one weedy youth, demonstrably foxed, who was playing his hand with inspired incompetence. Such expensive stupidity aroused no pity in Milord's breast; rather, he felt the stupid fellow deserved the trouble he was getting himself into. His opponent was a burly, red-faced man much older than the others at the table. As this worthy raked in the incompetent's last few coins, he was heard to complain

11

rancorously that if Callon's pockets were now to let, he had better vacate his seat for someone who could play and pay.

The weedy youth bridled at this summary dismissal, and was understood to say that he'd got one more thing to wager, namely his signet ring.

This was solemnly placed in the center of the table, and after a rather careful examination, was valued at five pounds, and duly wagered. The inevitable confiscation of this final bauble by the burly man having duly taken place on the next hand of cards, the youth was once more requested to give up his chair.

"No, no, m'sister has money in her 'ridicule.' I'll just go up and get it," whined the hapless loser.

Lord Randal's lip curled. Now the burly man would pour scorn on his companion and, hopefully, oust him with menaces. It would be something to lift the tedium of the most disappointing day Lord Randal ever remembered experiencing. He waited with some anticipation the casting out of Callon. Instead of taking immediate action, the burly man paused to stare at his victim.

"Your sister you say?" Since his speech was considerably slurred by the indentures he had been making in Mine Host's dubious brandy, the burly gentleman's speech did not sound as it is here reported, but rather "yer-shishter-yu-shay?" It was, however, quite understandable. Callon said eagerly:

"She's a poor little dab of a girl, but she does have some blunt saved up. If you'll wait, I'll get it!"

This was going too far even for a cynical misanthrope such as Milord Beresford, who waited for the burly man to castigate the wretched brother. Instead of which, the burly man was understood to say that if Callon thought the blond charmer he'd seen him with earlier was a poor little dab of a girl, he must be out of his head.

"Oh, *that* one's not m'sister," Callon hurried to inform him. "That was one of the muslin company who attend these meets in the hope of attaching a winner," he leered, presenting the veritable picture of a jumped-up mushroom with his affectation of a man-of-the-world air. He called a waiter and instructed him to desire his sister, Miss Chloe Keith, to present herself at once in the hallway, with her reticule, on urgent business.

Lord Randal was suddenly sickened by the whole affair. What was he doing in this miserable mélange of cits and rogues, pigeons and tricksters? He caught some vague questions about the discrepancy in the names of Callon and his sister as he was looking about for a table on which to place his glass. Apparently the chit was a half sister only. Milord knew a fleeting pity for the wretched little dab being choused out of her savings by a conscienceless half brother, but the matter, after all, was none of his business. He made his way slowly through the crowded taproom toward the main hallway, and finally emerged into its gloom—for the landlord had no need to present a welcoming light on this of all nights!—just as the front door swept open and Milord's opponent, the victorious Lord Peke, swept into the inn with two other men with whom Lord Randal was slightly acquainted.

Lord Randal drew back into the shadows, setting his teeth. It lacked but this to make today the worst it had ever been his bad luck to live through. Already he could hear the taunts, the drunken jibes and laughter, the mocking aspersions on his ability to chose a winner. Unbearable! For the first time in his life, Lord Randal ran shy. Fading rapidly into the background, Milord sought and found the steep and narrow backstairs, ran lightly up to his wretched shared room, snatched up his portmanteau, which he had not had the heart to unpack,

13

and ran down the back stairs to the kitchen and out to the stable.

This building, although grudgingly lighted by two lanterns, appeared at first to be empty. Milord made his way slowly past the crowded stalls until he recognized his own two high-bred beasts jammed into one single stall. This set his already precarious hold upon his temper quite aside, and he indulged in a blistering oath.

This was followed by a gasp. Since Lord Randal had not made the sound, nor had his horses, Milord was aware that he had an audience for his ill-temper. Hoping that it was a stableboy who could help him in putting his pair to the curricle, he peered around in the semi-gloom.

Backed into one corner under the loft he beheld a slight, small figure which clasped to its chest an untidy bundle of clothes. All that Milord could distinguish of the face was a small white triangle set with the biggest pair of eyes he had ever seen in a human face. "Just like a cat!" was his lordship's first thought, and then, as he perceived the garments the figure was wearing, "My God, it's a girl!"

The little figure straightened bravely and came forward to face him. She held in her arms what Randal was able to see was rough breeches and a pair of rather down-at-heel riding boots. Over one arm was draped a heavy frieze coat. The small pointed face looked up at him steadfastly, and a low voice said,

"I am compelled to run away, you see, and it is dark and wet and—cold—and I think I would do better dressed as a boy."

A suspicion was beginning to form itself in Milord's mind, but he really did not wish to involve himself in an imbroglio which might have distressing repercussions. So rather cravenly he replied, "Yes, well, that is

14

surely your own affair and I can have nothing to say in the matter. Pray forgive me for frightening you!"

To which the girl replied gently, "Indeed, sir, you did not frighten me! I admit I was a little startled by your—obvious displeasure at finding your horses so crowded. But they are a gallant-hearted pair, and are making do with their cramped quarters like the thoroughbreds they are!"

Much struck by this comment, Lord Randal gave the child another, more searching glance. "And how," he said, with the smile which had quite devastated female hearts in the Beau Monde, "do you know they are making do so gallantly?"

"Why, sir," the girl answered, with a shy smile of her own which struck Lord Randal as remarkably sweet, "I have been talking to them and giving them a bait of corn. Our host is either very clutch-fisted, or very forgetful. He had not seen to their feeding."

"You entered that crowded stall to feed Thunder and Lightning?" queried Lord Randal incredulously.

"They know I mean them nothing but good," the child advised him firmly. "I have an—*affinity* with horses."

Startled out of his normal politeness, Milord gave a burst of laughter. The girl did not seem surprised.

"Very few people accept the truth of my claim until I have proved it to them. In fact, I have made my living since my uncle died by working with the riding horses in the area where we lived. I have saved enough money to take me to London, where it is my intention to set up a school for the training of children to ride properly, and a stable of horses suitable for their use." She displayed a small handbag of the sort popularly known as a reticule. It seemed pleasantly full. "This was to get me to London, see me established in some moderately-priced, decent lodging, and support me until I can make my dream a reality."

"Yet you are, I believe, about to don a disguise and escape into the night," suggested Lord Randal, cursing his own stupidity in involving himself in the problems of a strange female, yet somehow unable to prevent the words. "I wonder if you might be Miss Chloe Keith?"

"That is correct," said the self-possessed child. "I have been aware since I set out from Grange Holt that to permit my stepbrother to accompany me was a grave mistake. Not only has he insisted upon stopping at every second inn to quench his thirst, but he begged that we break our journey in this uncomfortable place last night in order that he might attend the—er—mill which took place this afternoon. To make matters worse, he demanded that we remain tonight so that he might increase by gaming the small legacy left him by my uncle. I myself had grave doubts of his being able to do so, but he had already won a sizable bet on the champion this afternoon, and nothing could deter him from 'riding his luck,' as he called it, tonight." She sighed. "He has had a dull life, and I pity him, but I made up my mind tonight while I ate my dinner in the kitchen to avoid the high spirits in the dining parlor, that I must leave him and make my own way to London. To this end, I purchased the Sunday suit of one of the stableboys, and came down to take one of the horses."

Lord Randal, who had been smiling at this rather pedantic account of the child's circumstances, suddenly turned grave. "That, Miss Keith, was an ill-advised decision. Horse-stealing is punishable by—"

"The horses are mine," said the child gently. "Also the coach. They belonged to my mother. I was merely giving my stepbrother a lift to London."

"But can you prove that?" persisted his lordship.

"After all, you are a very young lady, and it will be judged that you are under your brother's protection. I regret to have to tell you, but Mr. Callon seems to have lost all his money, his signet ring, and may even now be wagering your coach and horses, if he has remembered their existence. When I left the taproom, he had just sent a waiter to summon you to bring down your reticule for his use." Meeting her stricken gaze, he added, "He is quite drunk—beyond reasoning with."

The huge eyes held his for a moment with dismay, and then the child said firmly, "I shall have to hurry, then, shall I not? For I must tell you I do not relish the thought of an argument as to the ownership of my savings with Reggie, if he is shot in the neck!"

Grinning involuntarily at the slang, Milord nodded agreement. "Which are your horses? I'll find you a saddle and get one ready while you change over there. Unless you would rather trust yourself to my protection, and permit me to deliver you to whatever lodging you have chosen in London?"

Whatever the child would have answered, Beresford never knew, for at this instant the door of the kitchen was thrown open, and the landlord and two other men hurried out toward the stable. Lord Randal recognized the weedy youth just as Chloe gasped, "It's Reggie!"

"Get back into the shadows!" snapped Milord, and went at once to his own cattle. When the landlord came blustering into the stable, closely followed by Callon and the waiter who had been sent to find Miss Keith, Lord Randal had already led his mettlesome pair out of their crowded stall and was in process of harnessing them to his curricle, which had been carelessly trundled against one wall out of the way.

"Now what's to do? Who told you to—" began the landlord, angrily.

Milord had turned on the landlord a glance so icy

that his words caught in his throat. "The local magistrate will hear of your behavior, Host," said his lordship, sternly. "Accepting full stabling fees for thoroughbreds, and then cramming them into one stall without feeding them! If they have been injured in the slightest, I shall have you up before the Sessions!"

Suddenly taken aback, the landlord began to cringe and make excuses, but Milord would not hear him. "I have no wish to discuss anything with you. My lawyers shall let you know what my decision must be."

In some alarm, the landlord signalled the waiter to assist his lordship with the harnessing. Lord Randal permitted this, but without further conversation. After a few minutes the wretched Callon ventured to ask a question. "While you have been here, your honor, have you seen aught of a girl?"

Lord Randal stopped what he was doing, turned, and ran his gaze over the weedy youth from his untidy hair to his muddied boots. Then, still without speaking, he turned back to his horses.

Embarrassed by this cut direct, the youth cast a half-hearted glance around the shadowy stable. With some difficulty he recognized the ancient coach in which he and his half sister had come to the inn, and saw beyond it the two horses which had pulled it. He touched the landlord's arm.

"My—my coach is still here. Perhaps my sister is spending the night with one of your maids. She was not at all comfortable in the truckle bed in the room we shared last night. Would not even remove her cloak." He turned and drifted back toward the inn.

The landlord seemed glad of a legitimate excuse for quitting Milord's company. He walked quickly after Callon. "Here, now, young sir, I'll not be letting you knock up the maids if they've gone to bed. Your sister will appear in the morning, I've no doubt."

The waiter finished his part of the harnessing and peered at Lord Randal. "Will there by anything else, your honor?" he said insinuatingly.

"Yes. Get out," snapped Milord, so fiercely that the fellow scuttled out of the stable without claiming the tip he had hoped for.

Waiting long enough to assure himself that the unwelcome company had indeed gone, Lord Randal said softly, "It is safe to venture forth! They are back inside the inn."

Close behind him he heard a small voice, "Thank you, sir! You have been a friend in need! I wish I might in some manner repay you for your kindness."

Milord turned to perceive a small and not too clean urchin in well worn boots and breeches and a coat a little too big for him. This grubby apparition was revealed to be Miss Chloe Keith only by the sight of the huge, anxious eyes and the bundle of female garments which she clutched to her chest. The final disguising touch was the small cap into which she had thrust her hair.

Rather reluctantly, for he was already having second thoughts as to the propriety of the step he was taking, Lord Randal said slowly, "I believe I must suggest that you do not attempt to remove one of your own horses from this stable, for I have suspicion that Mine Host will have one eye to the crack in the shutters to see if indeed Miss Keith might be attempting to run off with her brother's horses." He tried to smile. "So will you do me the honor, ma'am, to permit me to drive you to London? My horses are rested, and thanks to your care, well fed, and should not make too much of the journey. And since it is night-time, your presence in my company will not be a matter of conjecture or even comment!"

The child regarded him. Then she said, equally quietly,

19

"That seems to be the best solution of the situation into which I have gotten myself. My half brother has the direction of the place to which we are going, and can probably get my coach there with my luggage by tomorrow night." She nodded her head decisively. "Thank you. I shall be most grateful."

Deeply thankful for her lack of feminine hesitations and vaporings, Milord handed her up into the curricle. "It might be as well for you to crouch down," he suggested. "Uncomfortable, undignified, perhaps; but less likely to draw unwanted attention, don't you think?"

Her smile surprised him with its sweetness, as she deftly curled herself in a very small ball at his feet. Within a moment Lord Randal had taken the reins and guided his pair out of the stable and through the muddy yard to the road.

Chapter Two

A MILE OR SO along the road to London, Lord Randal pulled up his pair and assisted Miss Keith to rise and seat herself beside him. He had been surprised and pleased at the child's behavior—her poise and calm acceptance of the exigencies of her situation were far from what he would have expected from one of her sex. Perhaps, he considered, it was her youth and inexperience which allowed her to act so sensibly. More like a boy than a girl, he decided, congratulating himself that, since he had quite unaccountably placed himself in a position of benefactor, the recipient of his philanthropic activities should be causing so little trouble. With an ironic smile at the comments his friends would utter if they ever learned of his Good Samaritanism, he addressed the child pleasantly.

"I have your name, Miss Keith, but I believe I have not told you mine. I am Beresford. You may call me Lord Randal, and I shall call you Chloe."

There was a moment of silence and then the small voice said, "Thank you, Lord Randal. You have been very kind."

Was there a hint of amusement in the child's voice? Milord told himself to be thankful she was playful rather than lachrymose, but what cause for laughter should his name afford? He continued, "I have been thinking that it would be most imprudent to deposit a child, especially a female, alone in a strange lodging, so I shall take you home with me to Beresford House, where my housekeeper, Mrs. Tilley, will take very good care of you until we can ascertain that your brother has indeed arrived at your hostel. I expect this plan will meet with your approval?" he ended, casually.

"Perhaps not quite," objected the small voice, the hint of amusement now quite apparent. "You see, I cannot picture the good Mrs. Tilley approving of Lord Randal Beresford introducing a young lady dressed as a stableboy into the no doubt irreproachable halls of Beresford House. I am twenty-one years old, your lordship, for all I am such a poor little dab of a female."

"Good God!" was all that his lordship could find to say.

Miss Keith chuckled. "I thought that might bring you to change your plans, sir! I shall be most obliged for your assistance to London, and will warrant to take myself off to my friend's home without further imposition upon your kindness, at the first staging inn we come to in the metropolis."

For some reason Lord Randal did not at all find himself pleased with the situation. Most uncharacteristically he had put himself to the trouble of offering aid and succor to a child in a difficulty, only to find the child a young woman of marriageable, and therefore compromisable, age. For so wily and practiced an evader of all the traps and hazards of the Marriage Mart, this could be disaster. He drove in silence for several minutes, and then, turning testily toward his guest, said in a harsh voice, "I wish you had told me this earlier!"

The chit seemed to be awake upon every suit, for her next remark, delivered in a tone which set Lord Randal's hackles at the rise, was, "Sir, you do not need to fear me. No one but you and I shall ever know of your kind gesture. No unfortunate results will befall you. Be easy, Lord Randal, and let us get to London as quickly as possible."

Hardly knowing whether he was more reassured by her calm and sensible attitude, or appalled by her unmaidenly grasp of the situation and her calm adjustment to it, Lord Randal tooled his pair along the dark and exceedingly muddy road in silence for several minutes. A slight rain beginning to sprinkle down did nothing to add to the tone of his mind, and he allowed himself to sink into a depression. What a wretched start it had all been! The ill-advised bet, for one thing, which had set this whole unfortunate journey in train! The money involved was less than nothing to a man of Milord's wealth, but to have shown himself so far afield in judging the qualifications of a pugilist was a sad blow to Lord Randal's generally acknowledged *nous*. And then the sly mockery and open impudence of the landlords of those wretched inns, the disappointing mill, the rain—! And lastly this flight by night to London, with all its unpleasant overtones of the clandestine, since he was accompanied by a young woman in questionable circumstances. Milord groaned involuntarily.

His mood was not lightened by the chuckle of laughter he heard from his companion. "Oh, Lord Randal, do not permit your spirits to be daunted by this absurd business! I promise you, you have nothing to fear from me, and who else is to know—?"

"I should imagine every postboy and hostler from here to London," snapped the irate nobleman.

"That is being foolish beyond permission," retorted the young female, "for how should any such persons be aware of my presence in your curricle if we do not stop at any inns or posting houses?"

The incontrovertible wisdom of this remark did nothing to endear his guest to Milord. It might have been pleasanter to have had to soothe the alarms of a gently-bred female than to accept the implied criticism of this most unfeminine girl.

"You put me very strongly in mind of a governess my sister and I once had," said Lord Randal sourly.

Again that boyish chuckle. "Reggie thinks I am bossy, too," the quiet voice confided. "You see, I have had to get in the way of *managing* for myself for so many years, that I cannot take time to soothe ruffled feelings and sensibilities." There was a sigh from the darkness beside him. "I fear it is a sad lack in me."

Lord Randal had the enraging conviction that this creature was laughing at him. Since he could not think of a retort which might at once deflate her pretensions and indicate his own superiority, he forbore to reply. His temper, however, was clearly understood by his high-bred pair, who took instant exception to the harshness with which he gave them, quite unnecessarily, the office to get along. Plunging across the muddy road, they shifted the pole to which they were harnessed so that the whole curricle itself slid and slithered in the thick mud. With a horrid sense of inevitability the curricle caught against a milestone and tipped into the ditch. Unfortunately, Lord Randal's head struck against some random obstruction, possibly a large stone, and he lost consciousness.

Miss Chloe Keith was in one sense more fortunate. She was obliged to suffer a partial ducking in a ditch

24

full of rainwater and mud, but her senses remained alert. Checking quickly that Lord Randal, though unconscious, was clear of the water and unlikely to drown, she went at once to the horses. Whatever magic she was able to employ, she first quietened them, and then brought them to a sense of their obligation to their master. Within a short time, (having set them free of the harness), she had them back on the road and standing with unusual docility while she made a closer examination of their master's plight.

This was soon perceived to be very serious. Chloe could feel the rapidly-swelling lump on Milord's head, and his breathing was shallow. She managed to get him out of the ditch and leaning against the capsized curricle. Since the rain was now coming down heavily, it was obvious that he must not be left in the road unconscious while she went for aid.

Chloe brought one of the horses over beside his lordship. Cautioning it quietly against any sudden moves, she wrestled very hard to get the gentleman up across the horse's back. Although she was a strong young woman, and had exercised hard all her life, she found her strength unequal to the task. By this time she was beginning to have strong fears for his lordship's health, for he had not recovered consciousness. Glancing around in the near darkness, she noticed the harness straps. As gently as possible, she fastened one end around Milord's body under his arms, and the other end to the second horse. Then, with infinite care and coaxing, she led the horse to pull Milord up across his fellow's broad back. With a little sob of relief, Chloe mounted behind Milord's body, and holding it as firmly as she could, she directed the horse down the road toward London. The second beast followed as docilely as though Chloe had trained him from a colt.

It seemed a very long time to Chloe before she beheld

a light glowing dimly at the side of the road. It came from a lantern hung by a very small inn, and Chloe wondered with a thrill of fear whether the circumstance of its being alight at this hour might not be a sinister one. For what traffic could such a small inn be expecting during a dark and rainy night? However, she could not risk Milord's health with any longer ride in the inclement weather, so she slid down, and, stumbling over to the door, beat a lusty tattoo upon its broad oak surface.

As quickly as though she had been expected, the door swung open and a frightened anxious voice cried out, "Thank God! You have come quicker than we dared to hope!"

A middle-aged woman presented herself in the open doorway, but the relief upon her countenance was immediately changed to surprise and anger.

"Now what is this?" she said sharply. "I had thought you to be the doctor!"

"It is Milord Beresford who has been injured in a fall," Chloe said hastily, lest the door be shut in her face. "I am his groom, and have managed to get him here to your inn. He is very badly hurt, I am afraid, since he has been unconscious since the accident. He is well able to pay whatever is necessary to secure help," the girl added firmly.

There was some change in the rigid hostility of the landlady, although she was understood to remark rather shortly that she hoped she was a Christian and would not turn even a dog away on such a night. Much more to the purpose, she called her husband to assist Milord's groom and between them and a manservant, they eventually had Lord Randal stripped of his wet clothes and safely in a clean bed.

"Though there's little any of us can do for his lordship till the doctor comes," said the innkeeper. "Our son is

26

fretting with some childish illness, and nothing would do Mrs. Robbins but to send off for Dr. Wagnal."

"Lord Beresford will have cause to be grateful to you and Mrs. Robbins," said Chloe sincerely. "I have been at my wits' end! With your permission, I shall stable Milord's pair at once?"

Robbins nodded benignly. "You have done a good job, boy, and no doubt your master will tell you so when he comes round again." He took in for the first time the bedraggled state of Milord's servant. With a grin he added, "Looks as if you'd been dragged backwards through a wet hedge, my lad! Better come back to the kitchen and dry your coat when you've the horses secure. I'll wager you could use a drink, too! You look queer as Dick's hatband!"

"Thank you," Chloe managed to say through chattering teeth. Now that the fear and the physical exertion were safely behind her, she found herself feeling very queer indeed.

"I must not faint," she told herself sternly. "No one must guess that I am not really Milord's groom, and a boy. I owe him that for his kindness to a poor little dab of a female." And while she tried thus to rally her powers of resistance, she was more than grateful for the comforting presence of the two high-bred beauties she was making comfortable in the clean, well-found stable. Later, in the kitchen, she fell upon the bowl of hot soup Mrs. Robbins had set out for her. When she had demolished that, and washed her hands and face at the pump, Chloe went upstairs to see if she could help the innkeeper's wife.

She found the lady in the sick child's room. Chloe came to the head of the bed and scanned the little face carefully. Then with a murmured word, she placed her cool palm over the small burning forehead. Mrs. Robbins looked up sharply, but something she saw in the gentle countenance bent above her son gave her pause.

"It's well you sent for the doctor," Chloe whispered after a moment. "The boy has a fever, and it is making him very miserable, poor little one. The doctor will relieve his discomfort." She looked at the mother with her remarkable smile. "Do you sit down and get your breath for a moment, ma'am! You've been looking after the invalids and setting out hot soup and a dozen other tasks. It is time you had help. Let me get you a cold cloth to place on your son's head. I know it helped my mother, when she was ill."

Thankfully the innkeeper's wife let this very gentle youth bring the wet towel and place it gently on the boy's head. In a few minutes his restless tossing seemed to abate just a little and Mrs. Robbins was able to exchange a glance of satisfaction with Milord's groom. At this moment, a welcome relief for her maternal fears, a bustle at the front door heralded the arrival of Doctor Wagnal, who strode up the stairs as cheerily as though he had nothing better to do than to venture out into a storm at night. He was not long in diagnosing the child's fever, and prescribing suitable drugs and care. When he had in part relieved Mrs. Robbins' fears, he said briskly,

"Robbins tells me there's a fine gentleman come a cropper on the road, and waiting my attention. Will you take me to him?"

Chloe followed along quietly behind the doctor, and found that the landlord and his servant were keeping vigil by Lord Randal's bed. Doctor Wagnal examined the huge lump on Milord's head with knowledgeable fingers.

"He has not recovered consciousness since he received this blow?"

Chloe spoke up. "No, sir."

28

"How came he by the knock?"

"He was springing his horses," confessed Chloe, "and something frightened them. They plunged, and the curricle slipped sideways in the mud. I believe his lordship's head struck a rock as he fell."

"Hmm." Doctor Wagnal's bright eyes took in the grubby and unfashionable figure of Milord's groom, but he said nothing, only returning to subject the limp figure on the bed to a searching examination. In the middle of this, he seemed to become aware of his interested audience. "Thank you all," he said crisply. "I shall require the services of only one person from now on—perhaps you, Robbins. The rest of you may return to whatever you were doing. I shall speak to you further about Teddy before I leave, Mrs. Robbins."

Chloe found herself outside Milord's room. The yawning servant, sent to bed by his mistress, took himself off. Mrs. Robbins beckoned Chloe to follow her to her son's bedroom. The girl began to express her thanks for the care given Milord.

"You've been no trouble at all," the good dame interrupted as they stood together above the sleeping child. "A real help, in fact. I don't know your name, but I liked what you did for Teddy."

"Please call me Tiger," said Chloe impulsively, with a smile.

"*Tiger?*" For a moment on her dignity as though suspecting impudence, the innkeeper's wife found herself answering the sweetness of that smile. With a reluctant laugh she said, "I know the fine gentlemen call their little grooms tigers, but I never thought to hear it was anyone's name!"

"You are probably wondering how so great a gentleman as Milord Beresford could have such a tatterdemalion groom as myself, ma'am," explained Chloe. "I was being ill-treated, and his lordship rescued me. If he

29

decides to keep me in his employ after we reach London, I am sure he will have his butler dress me in proper livery."

"Mr. Robbins might find work for you here," said the good woman kindly, "if his lordship does not want to employ you—or if he does not recover from his injury."

"Milord will recover," stammered Chloe, feeling something very cold in her breast. "He *must!*"

The innkeeper's wife shook her head lugubriously, and then took the Tiger off to a tiny room above the kitchen, which had the twin virtues of being clean and warm. Indicating a pitcher and basin, she recommended that the groom might wash not only his person but his shirt, if he wished to impress his new employer. Then with a firm good night, she closed the door.

Chapter Three

CHLOE AROSE VERY EARLY and made the best toilet possible in the circumstances. She had hung the heavy frieze coat over the chairback to dry, and rinsed out the stableboy's coarse linen shirt. After she had washed herself carefully and dressed in the clean shirt, she felt better. She had neither comb nor glass, but ran her fingers through her short dark curls and hoped to escape censure.

She presented herself first at his lordship's bedroom and found the innkeeper dozing in a comfortable chair by the bed. His eyes flew open as Chloe entered, and he stretched and yawned.

"I'll leave your master in your care while I get some breakfast, boy. Have you eaten? No? Then as soon as you make him comfortable, come down to the kitchen and break your fast."

"I had probably better ride back to the curricle and retrieve his lordship's portmanteau," suggested Chloe, rather ill-at-ease at the idea of attending to the person of Milord.

Robbins being impressed with this notion, gave his permission at once, saying that the servant could take care of Milord until his groom returned. "For it may well be that he has some valuable items in his luggage, although his purse was safely tucked away in his driving coat pocket."

Matters being thus tidily arranged, Chloe escaped the sickroom on her errand. So very early in the morning, there was yet no traffic on the road. Within a short time, Chloe found the curricle forlornly tipped on its side, and just under the edge of the wheel reposed Milord's portmanteau, very little the worse for exposure. While she was strapping it on behind Thunder's saddle, a farmer came riding along on a cart full of vegetables. This rustic was pleased to assist Chloe to right the curricle, and even offered to haul it along behind his humble vehicle to the inn. More than a little pleased at her own competence, Chloe rode back to the inn ahead of him and reported her mission successfully concluded. Mrs. Robbins ordered one of the maids to set out a hearty breakfast on the kitchen table, and Chloe did it justice.

And then it was time to go up to Milord Randal's room, as the innkeeper and his wife obviously expected her to do, to relieve the servant of his post.

Chloe looked down on Lord Randal as he lay on the great bed. She had never really seen him in a good light, since their meeting last night had been in the ill-lit barn of the inn at Smoulton, and their flight had been through the darkness of the storm. She caught her breath at the pale, handsome face on the pillow. She thought she had never seen a finer-looking man. Above the white bandage which circled his head, dark hair fell thickly down onto a broad forehead. Dark brows slashed arrogantly across the top of a square, well-featured face. The heavy lids were closed now over the eyes, and Chloe wondered what color they were.

As that thought crossed her mind, the lids lifted and clear gray eyes stared up into her face.

"And who the devil are you?" asked Lord Randal Beresford.

"I—I am your lordship's tiger, Milord. You have had an accident on the road to London from Smoulton, and were knocked on the head last night."

"My tiger, you say? I do not remember you. I think you are attempting to run a rig on me . . . Did Peke set you on?" The contempt in his face was more than Chloe could endure without protest. She retorted, quickly.

"I don't know who Peke is, and nobody set me on to run any rigs. In fact, *I* am here because you took pity on a young woman in trouble, and *you* are here because you let your temper get the better of you and jobbed your horses, putting both of us into a ditch!" She glared back into his incredulous, challenging face.

"That's a lie, at any rate!" snapped Lord Randal. "What kind of cow-handed apprentice do you take me for—a young *woman?*" he interrupted himself as the idea caught at his attention through his anger. He raised himself a little from the pillow, groaned, and glared hard at the small, huge-eyed countenance above him. Then slowly the expression on his face changed to something very dangerous indeed.

"So?" he said, softly. "Sir Jerold hopes to kick up a nasty little row, does he? Something to pay me back for the ill-turn I did him in warning him off my cousin? Well, you can tell your employer he'll catch cold at that one! Now suppose you get yourself the hell out of my bedroom and send in someone to help me dress—"

At once Chloe's anger dissolved in concern for him. "Oh, no, Lord Randal! Doctor Wagnal ordered that

33

you were to be kept very quiet. Mrs. Robbins will be here directly with some food, if you feel hunger, but you must not jeopardize your health—!"

Her evident distress checked the furious comment on his lips. Putting one hand to his aching forehead, he felt cautiously at the bandage there.

"There has been an accident," he admitted. "At least you are not lying about that. Did you or Peke cause it?"

"No, Milord."

The faintest hint of amusement sounded in the quiet voice. "Where had he heard just that soft, laughing note before?" Milord wondered. The creature beside him, dressed in scrubby clothing and with a head of tousled dark curls, was saying softly,

"I swear to you, Lord Randal, that you rescued me from a very unpleasant situation at Smoulton last night. My stepbrother was badly foxed and threatening to wager my savings in a card game. You graciously offered me the courtesy of a ride to London in your curricle. It transpired, however, that when you made the offer you believed me to be little more than a child. Upon discovering that you had landed yourself with a woman of twenty-one, you were so—so *moved* that you rather lost control and savaged the reins on your pair. Since the curricle, depending as it does for its stability on the single heavy pole to which the horses are harnessed, is not the best balanced of vehicles, their instantly-taken exception to your unusual heavy-handedness caused them to lunge and rear, thus sliding the curricle through the mud into the ditch. And I should have thought," the amazing creature concluded her pendantic little explanation, "that you would have maintained enough control not to startle such obviously mettlesome, high-bred cattle! I am sure you must be a superior whip, to be able to handle Thunder and Lightning in the general way," she added, kindly.

Lord Randal frowned. "Shall we leave my capabilities as a whip to a more leisurely occasion? I am constrained to accept that there has been an accident. I am not gullible enough to accept you, with your wretched appearance and your finicking command of the language, as anything but a very queer bird indeed! But if in truth you are not some sort of gull-catcher, suppose you begin at the beginning and explain to me what this is all about."

Five minutes later, his lordship fell back on his pillows with a groan. "If I am to believe you, I am a nobleman who has placed himself in an equivocal position through his own stupidity! Now what is to be done? You say this medico has promised to return today?"

"Mrs. Robbins expects him within the hour," said Chloe. "You must tell him that you have lost your memory. He may be able to help you recover it," she ended hopefully.

"Meanwhile, we are faced with the problem of you," grumbled Milord petulantly.

"Can we not continue with the harmless fable that I am your honor's tiger?" asked the girl, in a creditable imitation of a stableboy's whine.

"No, for no one who knows me would believe that any servant of mine would appear dressed in—in whatever that outfit is you have on." His lordship's fine nostrils curled disdainfully.

"But none of the bloods or dandies who are blessed with the honor of your acquaintance would be at all likely to stay at this very modest hostelry," objected the girl.

"And that is another thing," announced Milord in the manner of one rehearsing a grievance. "Must you talk as though you had swallowed a dictionary? What kind of riding teacher are you? You sound more like a shabby-genteel govere ss than a legitimate instructor in equitation." He paused ruefully at her charming gurgle of laughter. "Fiend take you, girl, you've got me sounding as bad as yourself!"

"Worse," said the graceless female, still chuckling. "I should think *mealy-mouthed* would be a fair judgment!"

"I cannot allow you to ride behind my curricle all the way to London in that—that *garment,*" Milord continued firmly. "Not even a credit as great as I am sure mine must be could carry us through. Have you no other clothing?"

"I did have a dress and bonnet when I left the inn at Smoulton," admitted the girl. "But they are lost somewhere along the road, and in any case they were not much more fashionable than the stableboy's coat," she admitted, smiling at his look of aversion.

"Then we must trust that any persons who observe us will think you are some waif I picked up from a ditch," sighed his lordship. "Or I could just ignore you completely and pretend you do not exist."

"If you wished to be so kind, you could drop me off near the next village where the passenger coaches stop, and let me take passage to London. In fact, I must have been all about in my head not to have thought of it sooner! Now that I have escaped my brother long enough to protect my savings from his gambling fever, there is nothing to prevent me riding to London in the usual way!"

"Not quite 'usual,' would you say?" queried Milord sweetly. "That coat—!" He refused to acknowledge a certain reluctance to let this strange little creature slip out of his life as casually as she seemed to have rattled into it. He rubbed his aching forehead. If only his head did not pain him quite so viciously! And if only he could remember for himself the events the child had just recounted to him! There seemed to be moments during her recital when he recognized real places and persons, but it was all fragmentary and quite confused. Still, perhaps this doctor chap could restore one's scattered wits and set all straight. He sighed.

"Is there any coffee?" he asked, unconscious of how wistful he sounded.

With a little gasp at her own stupidity, the girl ran from the room and down the stairs. Within five minutes she was back, more sedately, bringing a tray into the room. At her shoulder appeared a buxom middle-aged woman in a neat dress and white cap, who inquired quite sensibly about his well-being, and promised him a visit from the doctor very shortly.

After she had left, the pseudo-tiger squatted on the side of Milord's bed and steadied the coffee cup at his lips. The first few sips gave his lordship a very queasy feeling, but Chloe encouraged him to go on, and by the time he had drained the cup, Lord Randal felt considerably restored. Next the girl coaxed him to eat a little bread, and poured more coffee to wash it down. When he had indicated he had enough, the girl removed the tray and brought to the bedside a basin of water and some towels. Milord regarded these mistrustfully.

"*Now* what will you be about?" he asked.

"I had thought to freshen you for the doctor's visit," said Chloe.

"Had you, indeed? Then perchance you should think again," replied Milord pleasantly. "Even with the broadest latitude, the duties of a gentleman's tiger do not impinge upon those of the gentleman's gentleman. Send Robbins to me, child." He bent upon her a glance of mingled suspicion and censure. Chloe maintained a calm, serious visage. After a moment, Milord grinned.

"Vixen," he said, challengingly.

The lovely guileless smile met his. "It is a relief to see your lordship so much restored to your natural acerbity," said Chloe.

37

Doctor Wagnal entered the bedroom to hear their laughter. "Good medicine," he approved. "Milord, am I to congratulate you upon the restoration of your memory?" He busied himself checking the significant signs of Lord Randal's condition.

"I—I am not yet quite myself," his lordship admitted. "I know who I am, but the events of the last few days seem curiously confused in my mind—shrouded—" His worried glance probed at the doctor's noncommittal face.

Doctor Wagnal straightened up and considered his patient, hand to chin. "You've a hard skull, Milord, and a healthy body. Your physical condition should be normal—that is, excellent—within a day or so. Your mental confusion may last a little longer, or may clear completely within the hour. Do not worry too much, sir. At least you know who you are, and you have a devoted servant who can see you safely home to your relatives and friends."

Chloe slipped away, unaccountably nervous under the shrewd gaze of the doctor. Could he have penetrated her disguise? Even if so, she consoled herself, he did not seem the sort of man to make an uproar over a matter which was not his concern, either as a medical man or a private citizen. *Even so—!*

She hurried out to the front of the inn and examined Milord's curricle, deposited there by the early morning carter. The vehicle, though liberally splashed with mud, did not seem to have suffered structural damage. Chloe went back to the stable to enlist the help of one of the lads in pulling it around to the yard, where she might profitably employ her time washing it down and checking the harness.

Returning a few minutes later with a stableboy, she was at first surprised and then alarmed to behold two gentlemen in a showy phaeton drawn up beside the muddy curricle, examining it with every indication of recognizing it. One of the two, a fair man with high color and an outrageously-caped driving coat, got down and strode over to the vehicle.

"It's his, all right! What do you suppose has happened to it?"

"He's overturned it, of course," snapped the other, a tall slender fellow with a coldly sneering face. "I hope he's broken his blasted neck!"

"Temper, temper!" warned his companion, snickering. "More like he's run down some hapless farmer or a Cit in a hired coach. I'd hazard a pony 'twas the other driver overturned."

"Then why is Milord's curricle here, mud-spattered and forlorn? By God, I'd give a *thousand* times twenty-five pounds to hear that he's dead or dying!"

"But you haven't *got* twenty-five thousand pounds, have you, Sir Jerold? Thanks to his lordship's interference between you and his so-beautiful cousin!" and he snickered again.

At the expression which now came across Jerold's face, Chloe understood for the first time the meaning of the phrase, "her blood ran cold." Her body seemed frozen, and she shook with a chill not entirely physical. Raw murder stared from Sir Jerold's eyes, and from the mirthless smile. Chloe turned to run.

"Hoy, there! You!" shouted the red-faced man. "Whose curricle is this?"

Chloe, entering the inn to warn Milord, said nothing; but the stableboy, hopeful of largesse, replied, "It belongs to Lord Beresford, 'im as got a wisty knock on the castor las' night in the storm! Blest if 'e ain't forgot 'oo 'e is!"

Sir Jerold descended from the phaeton in one smooth leap. "Where is his lordship now?"

Chloe waited to hear no more. Turning to race up the

39

stairs, she almost bumped into Mrs. Robbins, who was bustling toward the front door to welcome the new arrivals. Chloe caught her arm, looking up into the broad homely face imploringly.

"They are his enemies! They come to do him harm!"

The good dame stared hard into the little face with the huge, anxious eyes. Then, nodding her head, she brushed past Chloe, saying only, "Get up there and stay with him."

Thankfully Chloe ran up to Milord's bedroom and went in, closing the door behind her. His lordship, propped up on his pillows, regarded her hasty entrance with raised eyebrows.

"Is the inn on fire?" he queried. "Or is the tipstaff after you?"

Chloe ignored this levity. "The doctor? Where is he?"

"Gone to take a look at Robbins' son, I believe." Milord frowned at her. "What's to do? Are you ill?"

Chloe shook her head, half her attention on the stairs and the hallway outside Milord's bedroom. "Two gentlemen are here, coming up to see you." Then, catching his look of interest, the girl shook her head. "No, no, not a social visit, whatever they may pretend! There is danger for you! The one called Sir Jerold means you no good!"

"Well, here's a high flight," said Milord calmly, but Chloe caught the slightest betraying tightening of his jaw. "Am I presentable, Tiger? One would not wish Sir Jerold, whoever he may be, to find one *en déshabillé!*"

"He did not know!" she thought. "He could not remember the enmity which this man held for him!" Smothering a groan, Chloe darted to the bed. She caught at the top sheet, pulling it over the counterpane, tucking both neatly across his bare chest. As her fingers touched his skin, they trembled slightly. Milord watched her enigmatically. The girl glanced quickly at his face

40

and hair. Gently she straightened the truant black lock which fell over the bandage.

"Do I pass muster, Tiger?" he asked, smiling.

Chloe was very conscious of the red blood flooding her face, and stepped away from the bed. "You are— beautiful."

"Good God!" said his lordship, revolted.

There was a sharp knock on the door. Then, without waiting for an invitation, Sir Jerold Peke entered the bedroom, closely followed by his red-faced companion.

Milord Randal raised cool, arrogant eyes to scrutinize them. "Do I know you, gentlemen? What do you wish with me?"

Chapter Four

"IT IS REASSURING to find you here, Lord Randal," said Sir Jerold smoothly.

"Reassuring?"

"One would regret having to believe that so famous a sportsman would run shy on a wager," smiled Sir Jerold. "I was sure there must have been—an accident."

Lord Randal's eyebrows rose a fraction. "I had a wager with you, sir? How odd."

The color left Sir Jerold's long, saturnine face, and white-lipped, he moved a step nearer to the bed. "Odd? That you should wager with me? How am I to take that, sir?"

Chloe had moved swiftly to the head of Lord Randal's bed, to place herself between her master and his guest. His lordship lifted a cautionary hand at her.

"Why, sir, I only meant that I do not recall your acquaintance! What else could I mean?" He smiled tauntingly. "You may have been told that I suffered a spill last night in the storm. I am—ah—having difficulty remembering . . . some things. I did ask you who you were as you entered, did I not? Will you give me your name and style?"

Jerold gritted his teeth. "What demmed high-nosed trick is this, Beresford? Not two weeks ago you were familiar enough, warning me off your cousin—!"

"Now why should I do that, I wonder?" mused Milord, smiling faintly. "Er—what were my reasons—did I say?"

Sir Jerold's companion caught at his arm as Peke lunged forward. "Before you get on your high ropes, Jerold, should you not consider that Beresford quite possibly has lost his memory—a heavy blow will often do it. And if he has . . . should you not refresh him as to the nature—and the amount—of his obligation to you?"

Incomprehension, deep thought, then a growing satisfaction flickered across Sir Jerold's narrow face. The tension eased from his shoulders. He framed his lips into a smile which tried to appear cordial.

"Of course! Not your fault if you've forgotten! It was a matter of a rather sizeable wager on the challenger at the mill at Smoulton village. You were—enthusiastic as to his chances."

"How did he do?" queried his lordship in a tone of polite interest.

Sir Jerold made a deprecatory *moue*. "Not too well, alas for your hopes! It would seem you are rather heavily in my debt."

"Ah, well! There will be other occasions! I must congratulate you upon your success. And what was the amount?"

Drawing a heavy breath, Sir Jerold named a sum so enormous that Chloe's eyes flew open wide, and even the red-faced man pursed his lips. Milord did not appear to be moved,

"Indeed?" he said gently. "I seem to have been very sure of my own judgment. I shall, of course, have the money sent to you as soon as I return to London."

"I would rather have it now," snapped Jerold.

Lord Randal smiled and indicated his position with a slight gesture of one hand. "I fear you have me at a loss."

"You refuse to pay? That will make a good story in the clubs!"

"But a story not widely accepted, I think! Only consider the source!" and he laughed.

The red-faced man chuckled and renewed his hold on Jerold's arm. "Now why should you high-tempered young bucks be at dagger-drawing? There's such an easy way to settle it! Sir Jerold, I'm surprised at your lack of consideration for your poor sick friend! And you, Milord, must surely sympathize with an ardent gamester in the enthusiasm of such a fine win! So let us draw up a note-of-hand for the amount, and Milord shall sign it, and we can be on our way back to our engagement in London." He spread out his hands with a smile. "Simple?"

Sir Jerold, dazzled by the prospect of this honeyfall, especially if Lord Randal was really lacking his memory, in which case the amount would be recoverable twice, was all smiles and good will. Milord was watching both his visitors with the faintly amused, faintly arrogant expression which so infuriated Jerold. At this crucial moment Chloe, in the persona of Milord's tiger, stepped forward.

"Not bloody likely! Milord's no cony to be lurched of his guineas so easily!" Her hoarse, young boy's voice roughened with disgust. "You're no better than road agents, robbing a sick man—"

Not even the red-faced man's hold on his arm could stop Sir Jerold in this moment. Lunging forward, he struck the impudent groom in the face with his clenched

44

fist. The tiger fell against a chair and slid down to the floor.

Milord had the covers off and his feet on the floor as the door opened to admit Doctor Wagnal, closely followed by Robbins. The doctor gazed around him sternly. He had been alerted by Mrs. Robbins, and found the scene before him ample confirmation of her suspicions.

"And just what the hell do you think you are playing at? Robbins, send for the constable! I shall give these men into custody—entering a sickroom and savaging the occupant—! Get back into bed, Milord, I command you!"

There was a little babble of talk as everyone but Chloe began to explain what had happened. Wagnal held up his hand for silence.

"I have no desire to hear your excuses. The local magistrate, Squire Rennie, will no doubt require you to explain yourselves at the proper time and place! For now, you will leave this room and hold yourselves in readiness to accompany the constable when he arrives!"

Without another look at the two intruders, Doctor Wagnal went over to Chloe and knelt at her side. Taking advantage of his preoccupation, Sir Jerold and his friend went swiftly out the door and down the stairs. Within a few minutes they had mounted their phaeton and were hastily driving away from the inn.

In Lord Randal's bedroom, Wagnal was holding Chloe's wrist and lifting one eyelid. "How often did he hit her, and with what?"

"Once, with his fist," answered Lord Randal in accents of self-loathing. "I shall call him out as soon as I reach London."

"Good!" Wagnal had Chloe's head up against his shoulder, and was administering a pungent medication which soon had her gasping and fluttering her eyelids. "That's better! She'll do now."

Lord Randal froze. The significance of the pronoun came home to him with such force that he felt he had received a settler on his own jaw. "You know—? It is that obvious—?"

"Mrs. Robbins thought it likely your servant was a young female. It is no business of mine, Milord, or of hers. It would seem the girl found herself in the middle of your lordship's quarrel. Women have no *nous* in such matters. You must instruct her to remain silent during any further altercations you may indulge in."

Milord relaxed with a grin. "I must deliver her to her friends with the utmost haste, before she gets herself killed defending me," he said. "Will she be all right now?"

"She'll have a lump on her jaw the size and color of a ripe plum," he said. "And a very sore mouth; possibly a headache for a few hours. No permanent damage. And as for yourself, you were out of that bed quickly enough. Have you dizziness or faintness?"

"No. Thanks to your expert treatment last night, I am feeling quite myself this morning," reported Milord cheerfully.

"And the loss of memory—the confusion?" persisted Wagnal.

Milord smiled grimly. "Non-existent. I played along to see what Peke and his ruffian friend would do in such case. I found out."

"It would seem you have an enemy there," mused Doctor Wagnal. "An unscrupulous fellow. Don't turn your back in his presence."

He helped the shaken Chloe to her feet and into a chair. "I will give you something for the pain, child. I advise you to go to bed for today. Then tomorrow, if no further complications arise for either of you, I would recommend that you get to your proper homes in London

46

with all speed. This masquerade may be dangerous for you both."

"You are quite correct, and we shall attempt to follow your prescription to the letter," smiled Lord Randal. "You have my thanks."

After the doctor left the room, Milord held out one strong slender hand toward his tiger. "Come here to me, child," he said softly.

Chloe tried to smile, but her face hurt her too much. She was understood to say, in a manner garbled and hampered by her injuries, that she wasn't sure she could make it that far.

Lord Randal frowned. "What is the matter with me? Wagnal told us that you should be in bed, and the first thing I do is to ask you to walk around! I am the greatest beast in nature."

Chloe smiled in spite of the pain it caused her. "Of course you are not! You have a right to resent my interference! But those rascals were trying to chouse you out of a great deal of money . . . and I knew that Sir Jerold hated you . . ."

"You are a very wise child," said Milord in a deeper voice than Chloe had yet heard from him. "If I had indeed been afflicted with a loss of memory, as I permitted them to believe, I might easily have been—er—choused out of a small fortune. For Sir Jerold had enlarged the actual sum we wagered by five—and it was too much in the first place. I was very badly awry on that wager, I can admit to you. Peke—annoys me."

"Yet it is his friend who frightens me," confessed Chloe. "Oh, Sir Jerold has the hatred and the will to harm you, but the red-faced man—"

"His name is Wilferd," interjected Milord.

"Mr. Wilferd has the brains, and the control over Sir Jerold."

"I shall heed your warning, and the doctor's, and

protect myself in the clinches," grinned his lordship. "Now, let us take Dr. Wagnal's other advice, and get you settled comfortably to recuperate from Peke's dastardly attack." He pulled vigorously at the bellrope beside his bed, and within a very short length of time—so short that Milord suspected the good lady had been ready and waiting—Mrs. Robbins entered.

"It was as well you thought to warn me," she said briskly, lifting Chloe out of the chair and supporting her with one arm around the girl's slender waist. "I sent Robbins and the doctor up to Milord's bedroom as soon as I could. Not soon enough, it appears!" She looked searchingly into the battered face, now beginning to show the dark-mottled swelling Doctor Wagnal had predicted. "Those villains! I thought it was his lordship they were seeking to injure!"

"It was, but Miss Chloe defended me like a lioness! Rattled in and told them off for the rascals they are!" smiled Lord Randal. "I have great gratitude and respect for Miss Chloe," he added quietly.

Mrs. Robbins gave him a reassuring look. "So too have I, sir," she said. "I wasn't born yesterday. I know one when I see one."

With this cryptic utterance, she led the slight girlish figure out of the room. Milord watched them go with a frown. All very well to prate of gratitude and respect, but what the devil was he to do with her, this odd, child-like girl whom fate had seen fit to cast at his door? Get her safely to her friends in London, of course, as soon as she was fit to travel. And after that? It would require the greatest discretion to assist the child without compromising both himself and her. Much troubled, Lord Randal lay back on his pillows and tried to plan.

Mrs. Robbins, putting the girl snugly to bed and

bringing cold cloths for her face, had no such uncertainties. As soon as she had attended to the bodily needs, she sat down by Chloe's bed and asked, "Where are you bound in London?"

"I have promised to go to a market garden on the outskirts of the city," Chloe began, eager to share her plans with such a sensible confidante. "It is owned by a dear woman who was my mother's best friend—they were both governesses in good houses. Janet McLeod saved her salary, and she had a little competence from her father, I believe. At least there was enough to invest in this farm when she retired from teaching. She runs the house, she writes me, and her nephew Roderick, who also put money in the venture, supervises all the farm work. They grow fresh vegetables and berries for sale in London. Aunt Janet has made me very welcome," she hesitated, and Mrs. Robbins caught her indecisiveness.

"And what will you be doing there?" the good dame pressed her. "Is there some thought that you might make a suitable wife for the nephew, Roderick?"

Chloe blushed. "That might indeed be in Aunt Janet's mind," she confessed. "She and my mother were bosom-bows at one time, and kept up a pretty regular correspondence. But I have another plan which I hope to discuss with them both. You see," Chloe went on, "my father died ten years ago, when I was just eleven. He was pretty much cast off by his family when he refused to marry the wealthy squire's daughter his parents had chosen. Instead he married my mother, who was his sisters' governess. He got a job raising horses with my mother's brother, Ned Brown, who owned a large stock farm. After father died, my mother opened a small village school, and three years later, married a widower, Mr. Callon, who had a son, Reggie, by his first wife. My uncle insisted that we all stay on

49

with him. I grew up working with horses, and I have—for all some people may laugh when I say it!—a real affinity with them!" She nodded her head once, decisively. "After my mother died, I was able to work regularly in the stables, helping Uncle Ned train his stock and even teaching children to ride, and schooling horses for them. When my Uncle Ned died, a few weeks ago, I found he had left me a little sum of money in his will, enough to give me the hope that I might do what I have always wanted to do."

"And what is that?" asked the fascinated Mrs. Robbins. So much excitement did not often come in her way, and she was enjoying every minute of it. Dastardly villains, handsome heroes, orphaned girls masquerading as boys—! Better than a storybook, and right here beneath her very roof!

"I have dreamed of having my own riding school, where the children of good families might be taught the proper manage of their horses, and the skills of riding," confided Chloe. "I could also help the parents purchase safe mounts, and train the horses while I was training the children. This I know I could do successfully, for it is what I have been doing, as a favor to my uncle's friends and the great houses in our neighborhood. So I had thought to take my money to London, and ask Rod to help me set up a stable, and perhaps even place an advertisement in a newspaper where well-to-do parents might see it."

"It seems a reasonable hope," agreed Mrs. Robbins, "if you are sponsored by people of good reputation. Perhaps even Milord Randal might speak a word for you among his friends—?"

"Perhaps," Chloe concurred hesitantly, "but I am not quite sure I should impose upon his lordship to that extent." Her eyes met the older woman's with an anxious look. "You have seen that Peke, ma'am! I would not want him to recognize, in the woman who receives Milord's recommendation, the groom who attended him at this inn!"

Mrs. Robbins considered this seriously. At length, with some reluctance, she was obliged to admit that Miss Chloe was right. With such a villain as Sir Jerold Peke, anyone who had any interest in Milord's good name must avoid even the appearance of evil. "But it is quite too bad that the wretch had to see you here," she finished glumly. "For it would have been a very romantic—that is, I am sure his lordship would have been willing to say a word for you among his friends, had matters been otherwise! Very grateful he seemed to be, I must say!" Then, noting Chloe's downcast face at hearing her worst fears confirmed, the good woman rallied.

"But had you considered that you might continue the masquerade? Set up your riding school and stable as a young man with the help of your Aunt Janet and her nephew, of course! I daresay many families would rather entrust the training of their children to a young man than to a girl. Had you thought of that?"

"I have not met that attitude in the county where my uncle had his farm," objected Chloe. "Those parents who brought their children to me seemed to have no fear—"

"They knew you, and your uncle!" interrupted the good dame triumphantly. "Who in London will have that kind of familiarity with you, or knowledge of your ability?"

There was no doubt this was a factor. Chloe's shoulders sank dejectedly. Would her slender hoard enable her to last the length of time necessary for her to establish a reputation—especially since her modest stable and school would be far from the residential centers of the great city?

Mrs. Robbins took herself to task for a meddling,

romantic fool as she observed the troubled expression on the girl's wan, bruised face. Rallying her charge kindly, she hastened off to the kitchen, to reappear shortly with a bowl of good broth and a large mug of sweet tea. She stood over the girl until she had drunk every drop. Then bidding her to rest, she left Chloe to her meditations.

Chapter Five

TWO MORNINGS LATER, Lord Randal Beresford set out for London in his washed and polished curricle. Milord's pair were shining and groomed to perfection. At Milord's side on the high seat was his Tiger, brave in a new smarter coat (made down by Mrs. Robbins from one of her husband's), and well-polished boots.

The innkeeper's wife had offered to fit Miss Chloe out in a dress. After consultation with his lordship, the girl politely refused the well meant suggestion as being too dangerous.

"For you see, ma'am," she explained, "as long as I am in Lord Randal's company, it is better for both of us if I continue to be his Tiger."

"But Aunt Janet—?" protested the good dame.

"Aunt Janet will not be shocked to see me arriving dressed as a boy," Chloe smiled. *"Nothing* puts her in a taking!"

So the little party set out, sped on by good wishes

from both the Robbins, and even one romantic sigh from the buxom dame.

As Milord tooled his mettlesome pair smartly along the road, he felt a remarkable sense of well-being. The recent storm had freshened the countryside, trees and meadows presented a sparkling panorama, and the morning air was fragrantly stimulating. He turned to smile at his Tiger. He found her large gray eyes fixed on him, and she answered his smile with a particularly sweet one of her own.

"We shall reach London in good time at this rate! Your horses are superb! I believe they are coming to know me," confided the girl.

For some reason he could not quite pinpoint, Milord felt a sudden sharp diminishing of his pleasure. He seized upon her final comment with a frown.

"How could they come to know you unless you were in the stable?" he challenged. "I understood that Dr. Wagnal had ordered complete bedrest?"

"Oh, I am an early riser," Chloe confided brightly. "I couldn't have remained in bed on such a glorious morning, with Thunder and Lightning so eager to be off!"

"You *were* in the stable! I suppose I am now to learn that you groomed them this morning?"

"Is that not what a tiger is for?" queried Chloe, her own smile a little shadowed.

Milord met the anxious eyes with a stern look. "Tiger in name only! And just until I can hand you over to some responsible person."

The silence stretched out. Milord decided he had been mistaken in the quality of the day, which now seemed rather drab and uninteresting. He shot a sideways glance at his companion. The curly head drooped forward, bent over the arms she had folded so correctly across her chest. She looked, thought Milord with some exasperation, like a five-year-old who has had its knuckles rapped. "Ye gods! she will be crying next!" he thought, and, disregarding an inner warning voice, he turned to her and threw one arm across the slender shoulders.

"Come, child, I did not mean to hurt your feelings! I shall have to admit that I have never seen Thunder and Lightning look so well, or step out more proudly! You must indeed have—an affinity for them!"

This handsome apology brought Chloe's head up with such a radiant smile that Milord was dazzled, as though the sun had come out from behind a cloud.

"My uncle was used to say that it was a gift—to be able to work with animals, understanding them, and having them understand what you wished them to do. My father had it, a little, I think. His horses and dogs were always so well behaved and responsive! It was he who first threw me up on a pony when I was very small, and until he died he worked with me every day." There was a wistful light in the great eyes, as Chloe recalled happier times. Then the lovely smile reappeared. "Your team are the finest I have ever seen, Milord. So responsive and—witty!"

"Witty? Now that is a word I should never have thought to use about a horse," teased Lord Randal. "It is the consensus among sportsmen that they have heart and stamina and grace, perhaps, but wit?" He chuckled at the expression on the girl's face. "Well, it's plain to see that one of the witty creatures has never planted his great hoof on your foot, or refused a wall to which you had already committed yourself!"

Her challenging glance melted into laughter. "As well blame myself for having *my* great foot in the way, or for training my hunter so badly that he is uncertain of what was expected of him!" she rallied.

The next hour was spent most pleasantly in a

discussion of techniques. Lord Randal was surprised to find how swiftly the time passed when one was engaged in an interesting conversation. Watching the animated little face under the unruly mop of dark curls, he was suddenly reminded of the last *Ton* ball he had attended, and the deadly boredom he had experienced in conversing with the ladies present, all of whom were much more beautiful and certainly infinitely more elegant than his present companion.

It was about this time that he saw, down the road, a small cluster of houses around a village green. The road there seemed unusually busy, with carriages and farm carts lined up before the inn, and hostlers, parading horses around behind the inn to the stable. The sight of the village awoke a pleasant hunger, and Milord said to Chloe, "Shall we stop to break our fast at that inn? It may be our last chance before we reach the environs of London."

"I should enjoy that very much," admitted Chloe. "The thing of it is, I have an enormous appetite, and must be forever concealing the fact lest I appear greedy. So unbecoming! It quite puts me to the blush."

They laughed together, and Milord decided that this was the most *comfortable* girl he had ever had anything to do with. By this time they were abreast of the inn, and Milord drew up the pair with a flourish, handed the reins to Chloe, and stepped down. "Put 'em up," he ordered lazily, and added, *"Tiger!"*

Not too much to his surprise, Chloe tooled the curricle smartly around the inn toward the stable, the horses obeying her signals as though she had trained them from colts. Lord Randal acknowledged the master touch, and wished, for one moment, that she were indeed a male groom he could recruit to his service.

When she came searching for him in the crowded taproom after seeing the horses safely bestowed, Chloe was able to find Lord Randal without difficulty. He stood out among all the rest, she thought, with his fine figure in its well-fitting clothing, the proud set of his head on broad shoulders, the quietly confident expression on his handsome face. She moved quietly to stand at his side.

"There is a Horse Fair," she began, and her eyes sparkled. "Do you think—?"

Milord grinned. "Could I pry you away? Of course we'll attend. There will be plenty of time to deposit you with your aunt before dusk."

They made their way out of the inn and followed the men and boys who were going down the road to a large, enclosed field. There was a show ring, where the horses were being paraded for the inspection of possible buyers, and they moved in that direction. Then Chloe found her attention caught by a large group clustered at the far end of the field. She caught at Milord's arm.

"What's going on there?"

His lordship looked uncomfortable. "It is nothing you would wish to see, child. I heard about it in the taproom. It is a—a wicked business."

Cutting through the lazy afternoon air came the scream of a horse in anger—or pain. It was a chilling sound. Chloe's head jerked toward it. "Oh, no!" she whispered, and ran toward the group.

With a muttered curse, Beresford ran after her. Overtaking her, he caught at her arm. "I told you it was a bad business," he said quietly. "The owner is a local squire with a reputation for cruelty. It seems this horse unseated him before a number of people he was hoping to impress. He struck it repeatedly about the head with his crop, and it finally turned upon him. He was barely rescued."

Chloe's great eyes were ablaze, and her small face rosy with outrage. "He deserved to be hurt! Taking his

57

embarrassment out on a beast he wasn't fit to ride!"

"That seemed to be the general opinion in the taproom," said Milord. "However, he's had the horse in his stable, undergoing a course of 'training'—probably regular beatings—and today he has him on show—"

"What?" gasped the girl.

Milord's face was grim. "Exactly. The idea seems to be that he's offered to sell the brute to anyone who can ride him for two minutes. The price will be one pound."

Then Milord caught the look on Chloe's face. "Oh, *no!* I should never have let you come! The brute is a killer by now, whatever he was to begin with. He's seriously injured two grooms—one of them hasn't regained consciousness. There is local pressure to—put the beast down."

Much to his lordship's alarm, Chloe was listening to him with almost painful attention. Was she going to suggest that he try to master the killer horse?

But apparently Chloe had not even entertained such a thought. Her questions surprised him. "So if no one can ride the horse . . . or no one offers to, this squire intends to destroy the horse publicly?"

"Exactly," Milord repeated himself. "I might have known you would guess, with your—affinity."

The girl glanced at him sharply, but his expression was not mocking; rather, it held a brooding pity.

"Yes. Shooting it publicly will be a form of revenge the squire would relish. He probably beats his servants—and his wife," said Chloe with disgust.

Lord Randal stared at her. "Odd you should say that. It was one of the comments I overheard in the taproom."

Chloe nodded once, sharply, as if coming to a decision. "I shall ride the horse," she said quietly. "And then I shall buy him for one pound. He will be the first horse in my stable."

"You must be mad if you think I will permit you to—"

"You have nothing to say in the matter," retorted Chloe, in her new, confident voice. "I feel I was *sent. . .*"

Milord groaned silently. "I should have known," he told himself. "Affinities with horses—mystical sendings! The best thing to do is turn and leave this place at once! Otherwise you will find yourself embroiled in a scandal the like of which has never hit London! Get out, my boy!" Instead of which eminently sensible action, he found himself advancing upon the group of men about the tortured horse.

Chloe quickly caught up with him. "You shall not ride that horse," she said quietly. "I can do it, and I intend to. You would be injured."

"If you think I am going to let—" began his lordship bitterly.

Chloe darted past him and pushed her way in toward the center of the crowd. He heard her voice, hoarse and boy-like, call out:

"I'll ride the horse!"

There was some laughter and a few comments. By this time Lord Randal was himself at the forefront of the crowd, and his first sight of the killer horse struck him breathless.

It was a huge black stallion, dark as night and terrible in its anger and hatred. The ears pricked forward on the small, beautiful, vicious head; the teeth showed between foam-wreathed lips. The large protruding eyes rolled in a frenzy as the horse sought to prepare itself for attack from any side. Around the long, powerful neck was a thick leather choke-strap. This ended in a chain which was fastened in turn to a stake driven deep into the ground. The stallion was bridled, and a heavy saddle was cinched too tightly around his barrel.

Lord Randal felt red anger rising in his throat at the appalling evidence of the treatment the stallion had received, for the splendid hide was criss-crossed with welts and cuts, some healed over, the rest raw and bleeding. And from under the saddle itself a double track of blood ran down. Milord's furious glance sought out the perpetrator of this indecency—the squire.

Chloe was already facing a huge, gross-bodied man in a modish riding coat. He was mocking her, but the people around him had heard her challenge, and it was obvious that he would have to let her try to ride.

She looked, decided Milord, an unimpressive urchin in Mr. Robbins's made-over coat. But she was clean, and neatly dressed, and she had voiced her challenge. Some of the rustics began to clamor for the show. Lord Randal set his mouth grimly and moved over close to the squire and the small groom.

"You understand, do you, that you've got to stay on the stallion's back for two whole minutes by the clock? That's providing you can even get on in the first place," sneered the squire.

"Oh, I'll get on right enough," sang out Chloe in her boyish voice. A number of the audience laughed; some even raised a cheer.

"She's winning them over, by God!" thought Lord Randal with reluctant admiration.

"But first I'll have that saddle off," Chloe continued.

The squire turned on her, scowling. "What's that? You want to make it easier for yourself? I'm damned if I'll let—"

"Do *you* find it easier to ride this horse without a saddle?" jibed Chloe. There was a general snicker. The squire's face darkened with rage. It was evident he did not relish the reference to his own unseating, but he was forced to concede that to ride a horse without a saddle or stirrups would not be easier.

"Perhaps you'd like to take it off him, then?" he taunted.

Chloe nodded. Milord made a motion, quickly restrained, to prevent her. She had forced this issue. She must resolve it in the best way she could. He found himself hoping very hard that the damned little fool would not be hurt too badly.

Chloe had advanced to within a few feet of the tethered beast. The great stallion became very still, his large maddened eyes fixed upon this new tormentor. The girl stood very quietly, watching the horse, making neither sound nor movement. The fine ears pricked forward. Then, with a shrill neigh the stallion rose to the limit of the chain and leather, striking out at the tiny figure before him with deadly hooves. The crowd surged back, frightened by the fury of the beast even though it was chained.

"I've had enough of this!" shouted the squire. "Get the guns and shoot it!"

"You accepted the boy's challenge," said Lord Randal coldly. There was a growl of agreement from the men nearby. They did not want to be cheated of the show, but Lord Randal sensed a new evasiveness in the squire. The gross man shrugged his shoulders. "So be it! I'm going home. If the brute kills any of you, you have only yourselves to blame." He strode away and disappeared into the crowds near the show ring.

Milord called out quietly to the silent Chloe, who had not moved since she first took up her stance in front of the tethered horse. "Come away, Tiger! The brute is maddened with pain! He will do you an injury!"

The girl shook her head. She came a step closer to the horse, which had not moved since his lunging attempt to strike her down a few moments before. He was panting, and foam drooled from his lips. Chloe stood looking up at him. Then she began to talk, so

61

quietly that the circle of watchers could hardly hear her words.

"My friend . . . you are beautiful, a fine fellow . . . you have been hurt so badly . . . I am sorry for that. I love you, fine fellow. You have been hurt and I am sorry. You will not be hurt again, I promise you. No more hurt. Only love and good corn and running like the wind . . ." The small monotonous chant went on, quiet, soothing, until some of the louts in the rear of the cicrle called out rude suggestions. Milord turned and glared in that direction.

"If any of you can do better, I suggest you come forward now and prove it!" This brought an end to the jeering.

Chloe had ignored the whole interchange. Her soft voice coaxed and soothed and promised, and the stallion bent his head to see better this new man-creature who did not shout or threaten or cause pain. In a moment the girl stepped closer. The great horse reared but did not scream or strike out. Then Chloe moved closer still, and held one hand up to touch the sweating neck above her. There was a concerted indrawing of breath. No one made a sound. Every eye was on the drama in the center of the ring.

Chloe's voice came a little louder, but still quiet. "Men, I am going to remove the saddle. Then I shall release the chain. I think you all should move back very quietly beyond the fences. I do not know what action the stallion will take when he is released. Go quietly."

There was a concerted movement away from the tethered horse. Only Lord Randal stayed where he was. His eyes were fixed on the two figures—the girl and the great horse.

She was still talking, low-voiced, and Milord thought he had never heard a sweeter, more seductive sound.

He could feel his own tense muscles relaxing as he listened. Then Chloe lifted her hand and stroked once, gently, down the sweating hide. The stallion trembled, but stood.

She said, "I am going to take that dreadful thing from your back, my friend. I know it hurts you. I feel the pain. Let me take it from you!"

"You'll never make it!" thought Milord. "It's too heavy—and too high!" He moved forward slowly. Instantly the great head swung toward him, the ears forward.

Lord Randal found himself adopting Chloe's tone. "I want to help you," he said gently. "I want to help. The saddle is too heavy."

Chloe did not take her hand from the horse. "He is a friend too. He wants to help you. He will not hurt you. Let him help." But the stallion twitched and shook his head and pawed at the earth with one hoof.

"Must it come off?" whispered Milord.

"Yes," Chloe answered. "I think the squire has placed two metal points under it, so they pierce his body when pressure is put on the saddle. See the streams of blood?"

There was an angry murmur from the crowd.

"But when you try to loosen the girth, will not that exert more pressure on the barbs?" protested Lord Randal.

"I think I can ease it out gently," whispered the girl. "He has been so wounded!" Her voice shared the stallion's pain. He twisted his beautiful head to look at her. She murmured to him, and then moved till she stood almost under him. Her small brown hands were quick and careful at the cinch, and in a minute the two ends fell loose. The horse shivered.

Then Chloe stood close and, talking quietly, placed her hands under the saddle and gave a mighty heave, jumping with it to fling the heavy leather up and off the stallion's back. The horse reared, but the tormenting object which had been giving him such pain was down on the ground. His skin twitched and rolled, and he snorted and sidled away to the length of his chain. Chloe came and put her arms around his neck as far up as she could reach, and wept with relief and compassion. The horse stood quietly, permitting her caress. Then, crooning her little love song, she moved to his head and lifted her arms to unfasten the chain from the short leather strap. The men in the crowd turned and ran for the fences and safety, but Chloe and her horse and Lord Randal Beresford stood together in a little quiet island of love and exhaustion.

With a long, shuddering breath the great stallion bent his proud head and rested his neck against the girl. After a moment, Chloe lifted her small, sunburned face to Lord Randal's gaze.

"It's over," she said quietly. "He trusts me. Now I must see to his worst wounds before I lead him to my Aunt Janet's farm."

Lord Randal roused himself to meet this new idiocy.

"Lead him—? You are going to try to fasten this poor brute to the curricle?"

"Of course not! I shall buy me a little mare at the Horse Fair here, and a plain saddle, and ride slowly with him on a rein. He will follow me."

Milord set his teeth. He had seldom felt himself so little in charity with a human being. Granted, she had accomplished a miracle; no one had been injured; the horse was exhausted but sane. Not content with this, she now proposed a parade down the highroad with a sick and potentially dangerous animal, on an untried mare. "I cannot allow—" he began stiffly.

Chloe faced him wearily. "You cannot *prevent*," she said. Just when she would have welcomed a return of their easy camaraderie he was coming the great lord on her! She had better put an end to that at once. "I am most sensible of the debt I owe your lordship—" she began formally.

Milord said a rude word.

Unforgivably, Chloe laughed.

Lord Randal bowed, said coldly, "In that case, may I bid you God-speed? It has *not* been a pleasure to know you!" and stalked off, stiff-backed, to the inn. Let the girl do as she wished! It was no concern of Lord Randal Beresford's, he thanked God!

Chloe watched him go with a strong sense of depression. Still, perhaps it was best to break the connection now, before she was more deeply involved. No one knew better than Miss Chloe Keith the unbridgeable distance between herself and Lord Randal Beresford. And the sooner that distance was physical as well as social, the safer she would be from making a fool of herself. She sighed, stroked the stallion gently, and began to lead him toward the stable behind the inn. She avoided the crowd around the Horse Fair, but a small urchin came tentatively toward her, his gaze fixed on the great horse.

"Be ye goin' to ride 'im, then?" he asked, low-voiced.

"When his back has healed. It is too badly cut now," Chloe answered, just as quietly. Then she had an idea. "Do you know if there is a mare for sale there in the circle?"

"More than one, I sh'd think," answered the boy. "Do ye want a mate for 'im?"

"I want something to ride," Chloe told him. "Would you go to the ring and bring me someone who has a mare for sale?"

The boy turned and ran back to the crowd. Chloe waited. The stallion stood, head lowered, beside her. After a few moment a man came toward her, leading a pretty little mare. The stallion lifted his head warily.

"My son tells me you wish to buy a mare," the farmer stated, looking askance at the slender youth before him.

"I have the money, and I like the look of the mare," said Chloe quietly. "How much?"

Chapter Six

MILORD RANDAL RESUMED his journey to London a little later than he had intended that day. He lingered over a rather unappetizing meal at the inn, refusing to admit that the hope of discovering whether one wretched, unbeautiful, dowdy little dab of a girl had accomplished her purpose against the best advice of persons more knowledgeable than herself, had kept him lingering in this very uninteresting little village.

Finally, realizing that his absurd and unsuitable Tiger had no intention of asking his aid, he called for his curricle to be brought round, and set out for the metropolis in no good humor.

The traffic became heavier as he neared London. Milord had no difficulty with his team even amidst a crowd of less elegant vehicles. He did however find his eyes straying ahead, and to the sides of the highroad, to discover whether there might be a very small tiger perched on a mare, and leading a battered stallion.

When he finally did sight the unlikely trio, they had been joined by another familiar figure, the gross squire, mounted on a savage-looking bay.

Lord Randal's first impulse was to sweep on past the group without stopping. She was so demmed self-sufficient—let her handle the brute! However, something which caught his eye in its one flashing sideways glance caused him to pull in a little further down the road, and, waiting for a break in the traffic, return expeditiously to the scene of confrontation.

The squire had one hand on the mare's bridle, and the other was flourishing a wicked-looking crop. As his lordship pulled up beside them, the squire turned a red face toward the intruder.

"What the devil do *you* want?" was his furious greeting.

"You are interfering with my servant in his duties," said Lord Randal at his most arrogant. It was a manner which had daunted worthier opponents than a country squire intent upon grand larceny. The latter huffed and blustered, and finally came out with a rather weak,

"Your 'servant,' *sirrah?*" in tones he hoped expressed scorn and incredulity, but which in fact came out sounding merely addlepated.

Milord caught the fleeting hint of a grin on Chloe's face, but his voice, when he addressed the squire again, showed no trace of anything but supreme indifference. "You have, I am sure, mistaken the matter. I have left the pound note with the landlord of that very ordinary little inn. I believe a pound was the sum you announced as the price for this beast?"

"A pound—yes, I did say—but this—this . . ."

"My Tiger," supplied Lord Randal, silkily.

"Your groom didn't ride the beast!" With an actual

68

grievance to assert, the squire began to regain his self-assurance. "So the bet is off!"

"Do you truly think so?" challenged Milord, and his voice was softer than Chloe had ever heard it. She could not see his eyes, which were fastened upon the squire's paling face. "Then you really must name your seconds, *sirrah!* I find I am beginning to resent you."

"Name my—that is, this is folly! You cannot call a man out for merely seeking to recover his own property!" sputtered the squire.

"Can I not?" said Lord Randal, and it seemed more a statement than a question.

"But—well, no! that is . . ." The squire dropped the mare's bridle and produced a not too clean handkerchief from his pocket. Wiping the sudden sweat from his forehead, he subjected the elegant, imperturbable beau before him to a wary scrutiny.

"You would fight a duel over a pound?" he muttered, incredulously.

"I would kill you because you cumber the earth," said Milord with a delightful smile.

"You are demented!" gasped the squire, pulling his horse back away from the curricle, with nervous jerks on the reins. "Keep the beast—and *I* hope it will *kill you!*" and he set his spurs savagely into the bay's sides and sprang away from the curricle.

"That depressed his pretensions!" said Chloe in a tone of guileless admiration.

"Getting a little above yourself, young Chloe?" cautioned his lordship, but was compelled to grin, and a moment later joined her in hearty laughter.

"Did you see the way he sprang his horse?" gasped Chloe, "I'll wager he's halfway home already!"

"I must say I've seldom met a man less anxious to name his seconds," he chuckled. "I only hope he doesn't take out his chagrin on that fine bay!"

"More likely on his wife, poor creature," said Chloe, sobering.

"Well, you cannot save everyone," advised his lordship. "You did an excellent thing in rescuing the stallion, I admit; and you have bought yourself a neatish mare," he subjected the pretty creature to searching examination. Then his eyes went to the stallion, standing quietly beyond her. "Poor old chap! He's tired out," said Milord. "You had better let me convoy you to this farm of your aunt's. No, don't argue with me! I know better than a little country mouse what the roads around London are like. Follow me closely, please!" With this arrogant order, he gave his team the office and they minced forward, dainty disdain in every high-bred line.

Shrugging, Chloe pulled in behind her domineering defender and, uttering soothing and encouraging remarks to the stallion, followed Milord to the Kindlewick Farm.

Chapter Seven

AT LENGTH, late that afternoon, when the towers and roofs of London were dimly visible through the smokey haze of the great city, Lord Randal reined in his horses. With his whip he indicated a neat green and white sign pointing to a wide lane: *Kindlewick Farm, one mile.*

"I believe that is your destination?" he called to Chloe, and then turned his curricle into the lane. Riding the mare and leading the tired stallion, Chloe followed Milord.

When the ill-assorted cavalcade arrived at the farmhouse, its mistress came running out of the door to greet them. Miss Janet McLeod was a tall, thin woman with a kindly, intelligent face. She was dressed in sober gray, but had pinned a bright red flower at the breast of her gown. Her gray hair was neatly pulled into a bun at the back of her head. Chloe broke into a smile.

"Aunt Janet! We are here!"

"Chloe, my dear child, welcome!" the older woman called out happily, then paused, taking in the great swollen purple bruise on her godchild's cheek. Her eyes widened. "What has happened to you?" she exclaimed, and her glance went to the tall, elegant gentleman driving the natty turnout.

The gentleman raised his hat and bowed politely.

"I am Beresford," he introduced himself. "I have done myself the honor of escorting Miss Keith to you. I am sure she will tell you all that has happened. Let me assure you she has come to no real harm. And now, may I bid you both good day?" With a smiling gesture and a firm, "Good luck, Tiger!" he drove smartly off toward the city.

Exclaiming at the stallion, enquiring about the journey, and reiterating her pleasure at the girl's arrival, Aunt Janet led the way to the stables. Chloe found herself so busy answering Janet's questions while she made the mare and stallion comfortable in the neat, well kept stalls, that she had little thought to spare for a nobleman who was probably only too delighted to see the last of such a troublesome responsibility as herself. She decided to wait until she was in bed that night before going over the events of the last few days, and coming to some reasonable sense of acceptance of the fact that she, Chloe Keith, could never mean anything to Lord Randal Beresford.

There was much to divert her mind from her own problems. She found herself staring around at what Aunt Janet had been pleased to call "my farm." Neat green paddocks, white-fenced, stretched away on either side of the big, white-painted dwelling, two stories high—a very elegant farmhouse indeed. The whole place seemed remarkably well kept up, as were the large stables she had just been in. In fact, Kindlewick had more the appearance of a gentleman's hobby than a working farm. In the paddocks, lounging in the shade of bordering trees or cropping idly at the lush grass, were a number of fine-looking horses, while moving busily about the fields were several grooms.

"Aunt Janet! I thought that you had a small market garden," she said.

"Oh, that's at the back, my dear," Miss McLeod explained. "It is Rod's especial province. He has some very enlightened ideas, which he got from that man Coke, of Norfolk, who seems to be turning English farming on its head!" She smiled complacently. "Roderick has been very successful. It would not surprise me if he were able to restore the family's fortunes, in spite of what my pig-headed, pompous brother—May he rest in peace!—used always to say about Roderick! So unfair, but he was ever thus with anyone who dared to question his slightest opinion!"

Chloe stared with wide-eyed admiration around her at the thriving establishment. "I had not realized your—farm—would be so large."

"Rod is making a good deal of money for us, but that isn't his only reason for doing what my brother was pleased to call 'peasant labor in a foreign country.' " Answering Chloe's questioning look, she explained, "To Angus, anything outside Scotland was foreign, and therefore suspect." She glanced affectionately at the girl, her eyes taking in the boots, breeches and the landlord's old coat. "So suitable to dress in boy's clothing for your journey, dear," she commented briskly. "Now I must take you to your room where you may freshen up before we have tea. The maids have unpacked your trunks and pressed out your clothing."

At Chloe's expression of surprise, she added, "Oh, yes, that little snerp of a stepbrother of yours brought them here last night. He talked with Rod briefly, but refused to stay to wait for you, although urged to do so. Said he had no idea where you were, or when you'd be arriving. I thought it odd of him! Indeed, I often wondered what your dear mother saw in his father."

"Reggie probably didn't wish to face me," explained Chloe. "You see, on our journey here, he got foxed and tried to borrow my savings to wager on a card game. I slipped away from the inn to avoid his importunities."

As she spoke, Chloe had been following her hostess into the charming room, bright with chintz, that had been prepared for her. She almost bumped into her hostess, who had halted and turned to face her with a look of incredulity.

"Do you tell that that little mushroom, that counter-coxcomb, tried to game away your inheritance? It is to be hoped you've seen the last of him! But child, each word you say puts me in a fret to learn the whole. As soon as you are refreshened, do come down to the kitchen and we'll have a comfortable coze over our tea and scones."

Miss McLeod bustled away happily.

Chloe, hardly daring to take time to look around the pretty room lest it distract her from her duties as a guest, washed her hands and face and went downstairs in search of the kitchen. Janet greeted her gaily.

"Ready at last, dear child? I'll pour us a cup of tea while you, I insist, must open your budget of news. Reggie did not mention that beautiful man—Beresford, was it?—who escorted you here. How came it about? For I would dare wager his lordship does not put himself to that sort of inconvenience in the usual way?"

Chloe chuckled. "Do you want the whole tale in a few words, without roundaboutation?"

"Saucy child! Of course I want roundaboutation! Every tiny detail of event, nuance of feeling, and a verbatim report of all conversations!" Janet's kindly face was alight with interest and with the pleasure of having her best friend's daughter in her own care at last.

Chloe, smiling too, told her the whole story: Reggie's folly at the gaming table, her rescue by Milord from what could have been a very disagreeable and certainly a costly experience. Janet's rosy face grew even more flushed with anger as Reggie's selfish behavior was revealed. She became quite pale with alarm during the account of the attack by Sir Jerold, which had resulted in the bruised face of her godchild.

Chloe acknowledged her avid response with a grin. "You are the perfect audience, dear Aunt Janet! My little adventure seems a real melodrama when you receive it with such flattering emotion!"

The good lady shook her head. "If I know you, child, you will have played the drama down rather than exaggerating it. Just like your beloved mother—the most serene woman, so capable!" Her glance sharpened. "But that is not the whole tale, is it? I know how you came by the ugly bruise upon your face, but now how you acquired that noble, wounded stallion."

Janet was no longer smiling when the story of the savagely tormented horse was finished. Without comment, she got up and made a fresh pot of tea. After pouring them both a cup, she sipped slowly. Then she said, "You might have been killed, my child."

"No," said Chloe quietly.

"Yet in his pain, driven to madness by his torment, the horse might have trampled you without personal spite . . ."

"I think not," said Chloe gently. "You see—we had communicated, he and I. He knew I had come to help him."

Janet shook her head. "At least he *did* not hurt you,"

she admitted. "He seems a noble beast. Rod will be impressed."

"How is your nephew?" asked Chloe. "And also, where is he? I hope he is not too angry with you for foisting me and my animals onto him?"

Janet smiled complacently. "He has gone to see if he can get pupils for your new riding school. He did want to have something positive to present to you when you came."

"Kind Rod," smiled Chloe. "I remember him from that one visit. Such a solemn, quiet little boy he was!"

"He is still solemn and quiet," said Janet. "Now, upstairs to your bedroom, dear Chloe, and rest and refresh yourself. I'll just see to supper and then come up to help you put away your clothing."

"I believe I must buy a few clothes," frowned Chloe. "I wonder, Aunt Janet, if it would help my chances at establishing the riding school if I pretended to be a young man and dressed accordingly?"

Janet did this madcap suggestion the courtesy of considering it carefully. "The initial advantage might be greater," she decided finally, "but in the long run, it would prove irksome to be forever minding your conversation and sustaining the characterization. And the resultant brouhaha if the masquerade were to be discovered might likely ruin your whole enterprise. No, I think you had best continue as Chloe Keith— even if it is necessary to proceed more slowly in building the clientele."

Chloe hugged the tall figure. "You are a tower of strength," she told Janet. "I am so glad I have your love and support!"

"That Reggie!" scolded the older woman. "I had thought he might protect and help you on the journey! But where is he when you need him?"

"Far away, I hope," answered Chloe dryly. "I do

better when I do not have to concern myself over his foolish starts." She frowned. "I hope he will go on more sensibly in London."

"More likely he'll be courting disaster," said Janet crisply. "All I can hope is that he'll be afraid to show his front here again! I'll read him the Riot Act if he does appear, I promise you!" She patted the girl on the shoulder. "Off with you, my dear, and rest. Dinner will be a wee while yet."

Alone in the pretty room, Chloe wiped away a tear of gratitude for the loving warmth of the welcome. Then briskly she put away the few things from her portmanteau, grateful that Reggie had had the decency to deliver her trunk and boxes. Thankfully she removed the boy's clothing, and placed it in the bottom of the chest of drawers. After she had bathed herself, she decided to try out the comfort of the bed which looked so enticing. She donned her well-worn robe and lay down. Two minutes later she was fast asleep.

She wakened with the knowledge that there was someone in the room. Lying in drowsy comfort, eyes still closed, she thought that a knocking on the door had first roused her from slumber. The girl stretched lazily, then flashed her eyes open as she heard a muttered phrase in a man's voice.

Towering over the bed was the biggest man she had ever seen. Even Milord Beresford, for all his inches, was not so tall nor so broad. Her eyes sought out his face. Beneath a thatch of blond curls was a strong tanned face, with bright blue eyes, and at the moment, a rather sardonic expression.

"Startled you, did I, love?" he inquired in a deep voice laced with amusement. Chloe noticed that he did not apologize for wakening her, nor for his presence in her room. "But surely, in such an old friend as myself, you can excuse my eagerness for a reunion?" And now the note of mockery in the voice was apparent.

Chloe regarded his complacent smirk with the mild benevolence which an elderly aunt might assume toward a youthful nephew.

"I do believe you must be young Master Rod!" her voice expressed gentle wonder. "Aunt Janet warned me you were still the solemn, quiet lad I had once met. It would seem she does not know the whole."

"About either of us?"

Throwing back his head to show a strong rounded neck, Rod shouted with laughter. "You are still the same little wasp I remembered—just a little better padded in all the right places," and the bright blue eyes swept shamelessly over Chloe's small form stretched out on the bed.

"Time, and past time, to remedy that," decided Chloe. With a lithe movement she swung herself to her feet. The trouble was that Rod didn't have the courtesy to move backward to give her room, and she found herself pressing against the huge body. Quickly turning her face toward his, she said sharply, "What are you playing at?"

He stepped back a pace, still smiling wickedly.

"Believe me, love, it was irresistible! Had you thought to find some rustic clod to greet you? With an aunt like Janet, former governess to a Duke's family, I'll be bound I'm as well schooled as any wealthy Cit's cub—or any fine lordling."

Chloe smiled. "Knowing Janet, probably better! But I would wager a packet you didn't learn that cozening boldness from Aunt Janet! Doing it a bit too brown, Rod!"

The giant cocked his head and regarded her quizzically. "I might have said you hadn't changed a bit, little wasp, but I'm not so sure of it. There's an enticement under the sting . . . Well, we shall have to see, shan't we?" and he held out a huge hand toward her. "Friends—for old times' sake?"

Chloe placed her small hardened palm against his. "Truce," she amended warily. "For Aunt Janet's sake." She was not at all sure she was going to like the man Rod had grown into.

Rod grinned at her. "That will suit me for now," he said, outrageously. "Come along then, love, and tidy yourself up. Janet expects us for dinner, and she's made a good one. Bustle about!" and still grinning, he went out of her room.

"Really!" the girl thought, "anything farther from a rustic clod would be hard to discover!" She'd have to watch herself with Rod, just as she had had to do with the younger sons of some of the local gentry she had worked for at Grange Holt. Well, she had manged it there; surely she could handle one man with a wicked gleam in his eyes and more assurance than was seemly!

She found herself, however, making a much more careful toilette than she might have done for a dinner with Aunt Janet. When she ventured down the stairs twenty minutes later, she knew she had never looked better. She was wearing her best shirtwaist, somewhat to her own surprise, and had brushed her short dark curls until they shone. The waist had long sleeves, which cleverly covered her tanned, rather thin arms, and a perky little ruff-like collar that set the small, big-eyed face off as though it were in a frame. She had no powder to cover the bruise, but the swelling had gone down.

Janet received her with warmth, and directed Rod to pull out her chair for her to the right of her own. "I understand you two have already met?"

"The half was not told me," retorted Chloe, grimly.

Rod grinned as he seated himself directly across the table from the girl. Aunt Janet hastened to defend herself. "Well, I did say he was still solemn and quiet—" she began, smiling.

"That's what I said. I was seriously misinformed." ·

"Oh, dear!" Janet looked with mock dismay from the girl's stern face to the smiling self-assurance of the big man.

Rod's gaze moved over Chloe's face and hair, and down her body as far as the table revealed it. "That's a very pretty gown, love. The color brings out the anger in your face."

"Rod!" gasped Janet, and turned to the girl beside her.

"Not quite as well as that *homespun* coat suits you," retorted Chloe with sugary sweetness.

Janet stared from one to the other, a real frown on her forehead. Chloe pulled herself together quickly. This feud or whatever it was between herself and Rod must not be permitted to hurt Aunt Janet, whose kindness and affection for herself was of too long standing, and so well-proved by her current invitation to share her home and all its facilities. So, smiling more naturally, she leaned over and caught at the older woman's hand.

"Dear Aunt Janet, forgive me, please. I am tired from my—adventure, and acting cross as crabs." She turned to face the man. "Will you forgive me too, Rod? I understand from Janet that I have you to thank for your efforts to get me pupils. That was most helpful of you!"

"Trying to turn me up sweet, love?" mocked Rod. "Aunt Janet, what was that aphorism you had me learn? 'Gratitude is the lively appreciation of favors still to come?' "

Into the stunned silence that fell after this set down,

even Janet did not seem to be able to thrust a well-meaning mitigation. Chloe ate her dinner, eyes to her plate, for several minutes, and then, feeling that she might lose what she had eaten if she were forced to remain longer at this table, she rose and said gently to her hostess,

"Dear Aunt Janet, I find I am more exhausted than I had realized. I'll just go up to my room now, take a potion, and get a good night's sleep. Thank you for everything! We'll talk tomorrow," and she bent swiftly and kissed the older woman's cheek.

Once out of the dining room, she ran quickly up the stair and into the bedroom Janet had prepared for her. Hastily, almost with loathing, she thrust off the rosy waist in which she had hoped to make them think she was pretty. What folly! Reggie had told her often enough what a poor little dab of a woman she was—in fact, it was a constant theme of his. Better to accept the truth of it and concentrate her strength upon the work of establishing herself with the riding school and the training of horses. There she knew she had competence, ability beyond the common—the affinity with horses at which Lord Randal had been so amused when she mentioned it.

"But I *do!*" she said aloud, in a tight, desperate voice which she did not recognize as her own. She wondered if it would be necessary for her to seek out new lodgings. She knew that Rod lived with his aunt, carrying the complete responsibility for farm and stable; could Chloe endure staying under a roof which was at least half his? Eating food which his work had put upon the table? She did not think she could bear it, if tonight was a fair sample of what his attitude was going to be. And then a new thought struck her: why had he been that way with her? Even at their first meeting, he had not acted like a young man meeting a guest in his

81

home without prejudice. No, even then there had been something almost hostile in his challenging attitude. Wearily, she shrugged as she donned her riding breeches and boots, and threw a coarse shirt over the chemise she had been wearing. Tucking in the shirt, she slipped quietly out of the door and went down the hall to the rear stairs which led to the kitchen. Luckily, the room was empty, although Chloe could hear voices coming from the dining room. Stealthily she crossed the kitchen and went out the back door.

The night air was cool and refreshing against her hot cheeks. As she walked toward the stable, she realized that she would have to prepare a convincing story for Aunt Janet tomorrow, one that would make it impossible for the older woman to coax her to remain. Yet it must not be at the expense of Rod—it was obvious, in all Janet had said, how much she admired and loved this giant man.

By this time Chloe had entered the stable, and all her thoughts were for the stallion. She approached the box where she had bedded him down with caution, speaking low-voiced reassurance. She found him on his feet, and the soft cloth which she had put over his back, to cover the ointment on his wounds, was off him and hanging over the side of the stall. His lovely head turned toward her, and a faint snort told her he had recognized her. Chloe went into the stall, and up to the horse's head. He bent it to her, and permitted her to stroke him gently.

"My poor friend, are you resting any easier? I promise you, you will feel more the thing soon. You will be running and trumpeting and challenging every other horse in ten miles, I have no doubt!" she laughed gently, and continued to stroke his head as she tiptoed up to scan the wounds on his back and croup. They did not appear to her to look any more angry than when she had first tended to them—in fact, perhaps a little less jagged.

"It is too soon to tell, my dear friend, but I believe you will feel easier soon. Oh, my friend, it seems we have need of each other this night! I shall stay here with you," she promised, in a low, broken voice. The horse lowered his head with a sigh.

"I pray you will let me watch with you," said a deep voice just behind her.

Chloe turned slowly, so as not to disturb the horse. So close to her that she could feel the warmth from his body stood Rod, a look on his face which was different from that she had seen before. Chloe drew herself up and moved away from him.

"I think we have nothing to say to one another, sir. I am leaving tomorrow, and will try to keep from intruding in your home again. Or cadging for favors." She could not resist that last.

The giant was shaking his head, and he held one hand out to her. "Please, Chloe, of your charity, do not remind me of my boorishness—cruelty—folly! I was completely under a misapprehension. If you would in kindness let me explain—?"

Chloe studied the handsome, unhappy face before her. What new start was this? Dared she accept on trust any overtures from a man who had dealt as cruelly with her as this one had? The giant was watching her face anxiously.

"If you do not let me explain—and perhaps even forgive me—I shall never dare to face Aunt Janet again. I realize I have deeply offended, but if I could be allowed to explain—?"

Chloe sighed and her shoulders drooped. She leaned wearily against the stallion. He whinnied softly and put his head back to nudge at her shoulder. Rod watched this display of affection.

"It is plain that it was not you who wounded the horse," he began slowly, his eyes narrowed on her face.

"Had you thought it was?" gasped Chloe, head raised to face him. "If so, I can excuse anything you said or did to me! That any human could behave in such a vicious manner should place him outside civilized society! I was able to save him—!"

"So Aunt Janet told me," interrupted the man. "She also told me the whole story, which I had heard in a completely different form already."

"How is this?" asked Chloe. "Who else—?"

"Your stepbrother, Reggie Callon, came around to the stable last night after supper and delivered your trunks. He told me a story . . . I was a fool to believe him, but I did not imagine any man would so contemptibly blacken the name of his own sister falsely!"

"What did he tell you? No, I insist upon knowing what lies Reggie has chosen to spread about me!" insisted Chloe.

Rod set his jaw, but, after a moment, he nodded. "It might be as well for you to know what he has been saying," he decided. "First, he said you had run away from his protection with a man notorious for licentious behavior—" To Chloe's gasp of outrage, Rod answered, "Yes, Janet told me the truth of that, including your charming brother's efforts to gamble away your savings. It seems he would have gambled away the very coach you both arrived in, had the landlord not interfered—probably in a laudable effort to make sure you did not have the Runners down on him for chousing his guests."

Chloe smiled politely at his effort to lighten her misery, but she could not deny that Reggie's behavior had hurt and angered her. Bad enough to try to hazard all her slender store of money on his folly, but to

84

blacken her name into the bargain! How many persons did he intend to regale with this story? And if it should ever get back to Lord Randal's ears—! The thought horrified her.

"Did he name this licentious nobleman with whom I was supposed to have eloped?" she asked angrily.

"No. I do not think he knew, if indeed he believed his own invention. At least he did not mention a name to me."

"But how did he know about the stallion?" queried the girl.

He seemed to have difficulty in meeting her eyes. "He said nothing about the horse."

"Then why did you assume I had tortured it?"

"I must confess to you, Chloe, that before you arrived I had formed a very poor opinion of you. From what Callon had told me, I mean! All day I have been worrying about what I should say if you came here under the protection of your licentious cavalier—or what I should say to Aunt Janet if you arrived without him—"

"Cast off after only two days?" sneered Chloe. "The wonder would rather have been that any cavalier, licentious or not, would take up with a poor little dab of a female like me! Surely you must have wondered, when you came to my room and saw the 'scarlet woman' at last, why any man in his senses would bother?"

Rod's face was white under the tan. "I forbid you to speak so of yourself!" he roared.

The stallion raised his head and pawed nervously at the straw.

"Be quiet!" snapped Chloe. "The poor fellow has been so tortured by men that a loud rough voice can set him into a frenzy. You have not answered me. Why did you assume I had tortured him?"

"Having had this false report of you, I am afraid I naturally expected the worst. When I came into the stable with my own horse before dinner tonight, I saw the two newcomers at once. The little mare is a charming animal, and I petted her before I saw the condition the stallion was in. I wondered at the sheet covering his body, took it off—and was disgusted and angry."

"You did not give me a chance to explain, did you? Or to reply to the accusations against me? I wonder why. Are you always so ready to believe evil of someone you do not know?"

Rod set his teeth. "I was afraid of that," he said, between them. "When Aunt Janet had told me the whole story, and lashed me for my stupidity—my gullibility!—she said you would not wish to forgive me. She said I had created an intolerable situation, and destroyed her chance for a companionship she had long been anticipating. She said you would find some plausible excuse for leaving Kindlewick Farm tomorrow—and she would never forgive me for depriving her of your company and friendship. Was she right, Chloe? Can you not find it in your heart to be compassionate?"

Chloe's emotions were in a turmoil. There had been reason for his rudeness—Reggie had a plausible tongue and she had watched him talking himself out of scrapes all his life. He would have feared that Chloe's account of his behavior might initiate reprisals from Aunt Janet or Rod, and hoped to get his poison in before she arrived to tell her story. But as usual, Reggie was no judge of men or women; he was too self-centered to understand the normal reactions of reasonably intelligent people. Still, he had caused a very nasty situation, from which she was emerging with deep hurt. Chloe wondered if she could forget the scene at the dinner table tonight. She could forgive, yes. It was easy to

86

forgive when the whole truth of a matter was known. Rod had acted harshly, but he had, as he said, some justification.

The girl sighed. What it all came down to was the fact that Aunt Janet would be heartsick if Chloe left her home after such an unhappy experience. She lifted her great shadowed eyes to the man's anxious face.

"Of course I shall stay for awhile—" she began.

The man interrupted. "No, that won't do! You must promise to stay until the school is established and flourishing—or until I can be sure you have something solid behind you to ensure your living in comfort—"

"That may mean forever," Chloe tried to laugh. "At this moment I fear I have little confidence in my skills."

"That is my fault," said Rod doggedly. "My behavior has made you even more tired and unhappy than your experiences on the way to us. You must forgive me! Please promise me that you will give me a second chance to welcome you and help you!"

It was her tiredness that won the day for Rod. Chloe nodded wearily and agreed to remain. The next thing she knew, Rod had lifted her gently in his arms and was carrying her back to the house. She was too exhausted to argue with him, and permitted him to carry her right up to her room, where she found Aunt Janet waiting with an anxious face, and a cup of tea, and two hot bricks in a flannel.

Chloe smiled. "It seems I am to be pampered out of my sulks," she said gently.

Janet was rosy with relief. "My dearest child, thank you!" she said softly and kissed the girl's cheek as soon as Rod placed her on the bed. "We'll both make it up to you—you'll see!" she promised.

Rod stood quietly by the door. "I'll stay with the

stallion tonight," he told her. "He'll be all right now he knows you are safe."

As she dropped off to sleep, Chloe wondered a little at what he had said. For it was the truth, she knew. But how had *he* known?

Chapter Eight

THE NEXT FEW WEEKS were the happiest Chloe had ever known. The loving care with which Aunt Janet surrounded her, the interest Rod showed in her growing stable, and his knowledge of horses, of which he made her free, formed a warm circle about her days. Yet she could never entirely erase from her memory the experience of her first night at Kindlewick, and many times she caught herself watching Rod warily. It appeared he was aware of her continued distrust, yet he said nothing further about it. It seemed to Chloe that he did not really care how she felt, as long as she did not distress Aunt Janet. Even so, Chloe had to admit, as she tentatively accepted their support, how grim and loveless her past few years with her uncle had been. She thought she could ask little more from life than to continue to build her stable at Kindlewick Farm, and establish her school nearby.

When she spoke of this to the McLeods, Rod advised her not to be in too great a hurry.

"You have your hands full at the moment training your horses," he said pleasantly. "Don't rush ahead with the plan for the school until you have everything in readiness."

"For instance?" challenged the girl.

Rod grinned at her engagingly. "A roster of prospective students, for one thing." He chuckled at her crestfallen air. "It just happens that I have dropped a word here and there among my clients in London—" he paused provocatively.

Aunt Janet was as eager as Chloe to hear more. Rod smiled at their excitement.

"Is clients too pompous a word, I wonder? Should I rather say customers? Aunt Janet, you would know the proper term."

"I know what will happen to you if you don't stop tormenting us, and tell us what success your efforts have produced," warned his aunt.

Rod capitulated with such a friendly glance at Chloe that her heart missed a beat. "I have about six little lads and lassies whose parents have agreed to send them here for training in proper equitation," he admitted, and then accepted their excited admiration with a very complacent expression. "I am to tell them when we are ready," he went on. "I shall need to go over with you, Chloe, the steps you will be using to train the children. Oh, I know you have done this with success in your former home; still it will not hurt to be doubly sure."

Chloe struggled between annoyance at his arrogant assumption that he knew more about her work than she did herself, and gratitude for his quiet efforts to help her. Gratitude won, and she was able to thank him with a flash of her old, lovely smile.

Rod noted this radiant sweetness with narrowed eyes. "I haven't too much planned for today," he said. "Why don't you meet me in the stables in half an hour, love, and show me how you intend to proceed with your students."

Not waiting for her answer, he turned and strolled off.

"Love?"

Chloe, stunned by his use of the endearment, found herself with nothing to say. Not since their first painful confrontation had Rod used that mocking blandishment. Yet surely his voice today, with its faint, delightful Scots' burr, held none of the sneering challenge he had offered her then? Chloe tried to rally her defenses against this unexpected development. She stared after the huge, cat-graceful figure.

Janet watched that revealing little countenance, frowned and opened her mouth to make a comment. Then she changed what she had planned to say. "Walks well, doesn't he?" she asked instead. "I can almost see the swing of the kilt."

After a moment the girl turned to the older woman, a betraying blush staining the sun-burned cheeks. "I hope I thanked him properly," she said. "It has been a dream of mine for so long . . . and Rod announced his success so casually—"

"He is a very determined young man," Janet advised her. "I believe I have come to expect that anything he puts his hand to will turn out well."

"Could you—would you tell me a little about—about what he's done?" asked the girl, surprised at her own rather stammering request.

"It has been rather remarkable," confessed Janet. "As soon as he came down from Edinburgh University, Rod used his patrimony to purchase a large tract of land here on the outskirts of London. It is good, rich land. As soon as he owned it, he went off to Norfolk to see Mr. Coke's experimental farm at Holkham—a Mecca for agriculturalists, I am informed! Rod was able to consult with Mr. Coke about the latest ideas in husbandry. Then he went back to Scotland and recruited crofters from the villages near our old home—younger sons like himself, youths who knew farming from their cradles, yet hankered to live a more exciting life than was possible on the poor farms in those remote areas.

"He built small cottages around the perimeter of this acreage, and encouraged his young farmers to marry. The close proximity to London convinces the men that they are near the center of exciting events, and keeps them satisfied. Here their particular skills provide them an excellent living which they realize they could never hope to equal were they to seek employment in the city itself. They work hard and do well. As a result, Kindlewick Farm produce is on order from most of the great houses in London and the better hotels. We have no need to seek for buyers—Rod has deliveries made every morning to an established clientele."

"He planned and managed all this himself? How proud your family must be of him!"

"On the contrary," Janet confided wryly, "Rod's older brother, who is now head of the family, has washed his hands of both of us, saying that *Rod* has disgraced the name McLeod, and *I'm* little better for encouraging him in his folly."

"But that is madness!" exclaimed Chloe. "If they could see all this—" she indicated the thriving establishment.

"A genteel failure would have pleased Angus more," said Janet. "Now, dear child, should you not be on your way to the stables for," she smiled conspiratorially, "your examination by Dominie McLeod?"

Suddenly lighthearted, Chloe answered the smile

and hurried off to the stables, where the great stallion, she knew, would be impatient for her presence.

Her chief interest and delight in the past weeks had been the care and training of the horse, whom she had named Amigo. He answered to the name, and obviously loved the small girl who was his personal groom and devoted teacher. Since she made every new step in his training plain, and physically easy for his returning strength, Amigo enjoyed himself very much, and was coming to have a very good opinion of himself. He contantly surprised and pleased her with the quickness of his perception, and it occurred to her that an animal of his intelligence and high spirits might be capable of more than the usual equestrian training. As he healed in mind and body, Amigo was a powerful, proud animal, eager to attempt any new exercise Chloe presented. Stableboys, grooms, and Rod himself often marveled at the perfection of understanding between the small girl and the great horse.

This morning, Rod watched impassively as Chloe ran through her program of training and exercise. She used the mare for her demonstration, and the pretty, gentle animal responded perfectly to all her demands. At last the man nodded his head.

"Well done," he said, quietly. "I can recommend your methods and skill to the parents of my customers." He smiled down at the girl's flushed, eager face. "Are you too tired to go for a gallop with me now, love?"

The deeper red burned up into Chloe's cheeks. "That—that would be fine," she managed to say, with what she thought was a casual air. "I'd like to take Amigo. He hasn't had his usual exercise today, and he'll be feeling very put out."

The big man nodded again. "I'd be pleased to see exactly what you've done with him," he agreed. "One of the boys will rub down the mare. I'll get my gray."

Chloe went to Amigo's special box and made much of the impatient horse. When he was saddled and bridled, she mounted and rode him out into the yard. Rod was already there, looking like a centaur on his powerful gray. They walked, then trotted, then cantered along the lanes until they passed the cultivated fields and entered into open meadows.

"Now," said Rod, "show me what you have accomplished with Amigo, Miss Keith."

Amigo, knowing himself to be on show, danced through his paces elegantly. Rod was unable to fault him, and as the girl brought the stallion back to face the man, she touched him with her heel in the signal for their special surprise.

Amigo drew up in front of the gray, backed two paces, extended his front leg and bowed, with a nodding of his great head and a handsome flourish of his mane.

Rod laughed and applauded.

Amigo loved it, and kept doing it till Chloe stopped him.

"Are you planning to add *haute école* to his dressage?" he grinned. "Or is he too big and heavy for the airs above the ground?"

"Yes, I suppose so," agreed Chloe reluctantly. "But he's so clever and willing! He seems to be urging me to do new things every day!"

Rod cast a knowing eye over the great glossy beast. "You've worked a miracle," he commented. "Pity such a fine animal should have begun life with that vicious owner. Still, it hasn't seemed to mark him—except for the scars on his back."

"He seems to accept new disciplines easily," said Chloe. Then she laughed. "In fact, I'm not sure who is teaching whom! Yesterday morning Amigo was in such high spirits that he took off at a gallop when I led him out to the paddock. He jumped the fence, then turned

94

and jumped back, then came to me with the most quizzical look and blew at the front of my shirt. Then he went prancing around the paddock, running through all the movements I have taught him. He really is—a darling!"

Rod grinned at her enthusiasm. "So he wants to sport his skills, does he? Shall we take him for a run cross-country now?"

"Oh, Rod, could we?" Chloe clasped her hands together and regarded the man with eyes alight.

"You had better not give me such a look as that too often, Madam Mischief, lest I become even more licentious than Reggie's disreputable lordling," teased Rod, but there was a new light in the bright blue eyes which startled Chloe. Then Rod turned his big gray. Chloe hastily collected her reins, pressed her legs against Amigo, and followed Rod out to the lane which ran along beside the farm. In a few minutes they were coming into more open country, and they let the horses go.

"Fences ahead!" called out Rod, and set his horse for the jump. Amigo followed willingly, his powerful muscles seeming to relish the challenge. The two horses raced across field after field, taking the fences as though flying rather than galloping. Rod heard Chloe's triumphant laughter and grinned sympathy.

"Water jump!" he warned, and sailed over it with a yard to spare.

Whether it was her pleasure in the motion which distracted her, or the fact that she had not worked with Amigo on a water jump, Chloe lost her head, and then, inevitably, her seat on Amigo's back. While the stallion sailed over the ditch with even more to spare than the gray had had, his rider found herself deep in the water. Choking and sputtering, she pushed down with her feet on the muddy bottom and thrust herself to the

95

surface. The next thing she knew there was a sharp blow against her back and then a choking sensation as something grasped her shirt at the collar and heaved her out of the ditch. Struggling to turn and berate Rod for his rough handling, Chloe found herself looking into the shining black eyes of Amigo. As she scrambled to her feet, the horse neighed with satisfaction. Streaming muddy water, her shirt pulled out of her breeches and torn, her hair dripping into her eyes, Chloe was not gratified to hear Rod's deep-throated laughter joining the stallion's.

"Men!" she said bitterly, and limped toward Amigo.

"You looked—quite interesting sailing topsy-turvy into the ditch," Rod advised her, straight-faced. "Was that your idea of airs above the ground?"

"No, but it has given me an idea," drawled the girl.

"How not to take water jumps?" teased Rod, dismounting.

"No. How to treat a horse who thinks he's a clown."

When Rod chuckled again, Chloe pointed to Amigo. "Look at him! He knows we are watching him, and he loves it."

Amigo was prancing daintily across the field, mincing with tiny steps which ill-suited his magnificent frame. When he approached the hedge, a small bird flew up, disturbed. Amigo reacted as though the hedge sparrow were a fire-breathing dragon. He reared, rolled his fine dark eyes, pawed the air and uttered a frantic, shrill whinny. Then he cocked his head at Chloe and waited for her reaction. The sight of both the humans doubled over with laughter seemed to please him, for he trotted over to the man and pushed him so hard on the shoulder that Rod, unwarned, staggered and fell.

It was Chloe's turn to chuckle, and she enjoyed it. "Do you believe me now?"

Rod picked himself up. "I believe our merry friend

96

needs a good lesson," he said. "These buffooneries could be disastrous if so large a horse tried them on one of your pupils."

Chloe's face became sober. "I had not thought of that. In truth, I do not plan to use Amigo in the school. He would be overpowering for a child who had not had experience with horses."

"That's sensible," approved Rod. "Molly is a darling. And I've located two ponies and a promising young colt for your school—"

"And now that you have found me six pupils, I shall soon be independent!" breathed the girl, her face joyful. "It is all thanks to you and dear Aunt Janet. I shall always be grateful to her!"

"Because she brought us together?" teased Rod, rolling his eyes in the same manner as Amigo had done.

The girl chuckled. "No, idiot! And you'd run faster than Amigo if you thought I meant that."

"You are calling me a faint-heart?" challenged the giant, strolling lazily over to tower above her slender form. Chloe regarded the wicked twinkle in his eyes with alarm.

"Rod! What are you—oh, don't, you wretch!—I'll call Amigo!"

Rod swung her up in his arms as though she were a child. Holding her high against his chest, he pinned her hands in one of his great fists, and then bent his head over her face. The black stallion was watching, ears prickled.

"Amigo!" called Chloe, faintly.

"Not very convincing, love," said Rod silkily.

But it was not from the horse that her rescue came. Instead there was an icily cool voice just behind Rod.

"Miss Keith, is this lout annoying you?"

Rod's reaction was lightning fast for so large a man. He whirled and put Chloe down safely on her feet, and then confronted the aristrocratic stranger on the roan stallion. Rod's posture was relaxed yet wary. One look at him showed that he was not afraid of anything which the stranger could offer.

Chloe, seeing Lord Randal's icy condemnation, knew that she had to speak quickly before antagonism developed between these two men who had befriended her. For Aunt Janet's sake, also, this meeting must not deteriorate into an open conflict. So, advancing toward Milord's horse, she smiled up at his arrogant handsome countenance.

"No, Milord, and yes."

Lord Randal's rigid expression softened, and a hint of a smile appeared around his eyes. "Tiger, you seem to land yourself in a variety of provocative situations. What is that supposed to mean—no and yes?"

"No, he is not a lout, and yes, he is annoying me—but I am afraid I asked for it, so we must both forgive him," and she favored both men with her sweet, wide smile.

Reluctantly, the men's eyes met and, almost against their will, they exchanged a look: rueful male acceptance of female incomprehensibility. Chloe took advantage of the truce.

"Milord Beresford, may I present Rod McLeod, Aunt Janet's nephew?" Then, as the men acknowledged the introduction, Chloe continued, "I had just called him an idiot and a faint-heart."

Lord Randal laughed, and, after a moment, Rod joined in. His lordship said, shaking his head, "With such provocation I am not surprised he was about to do violence on your person! Tiger, when will you learn the proper conduct for young ladies?"

Frowning a little, Chloe said, "When I become a young lady, Milord—which is hardly an eventuality to be desired in my case."

Milord's well-shaped eyebrows lifted slightly. "Not?"

Chloe shrugged. "You know of my plans, sir. I am going to establish my school for riders and my training stables. There will be no time in my working life for the airs and graces of a young Fashionable!" She struck her hands together lightly, and shaking her head, cried almost breathlessly, "Oh, if I were only a man! How much *simpler*—everything would be!"

Rod grinned. "But think of the fun you'd miss."

Milord was not best pleased by this rather risqué remark. His only interest in the chit, of course, was gratitude for the help she had been in getting him to the inn after his accident, and regret that her rather pathetic attempt to protect him from Jerold's violence had resulted in a bruised face. Even so, he did not relish the teasing, proprietory attitude of this rustic giant. Half seriously he wondered how the yokel would strip. Glancing at him, he met the bold blue challenge of the other man's eyes, as with a grin Rod said,

"I've had a turn or two in the ring—and lessons in London from Tom Johnson."

Milord looked at him with new respect—and some speculation.

Rod grinned again. "Any time," he offered.

Chloe felt moved to intervene. "How did you find us, Milord? And what may we do for you?"

Lord Randal reluctantly abandoned, at least for the time being, his half formed plan to challenge the giant. "I have been thinking about you and your school—and, I must admit, about this beautiful creature," and he nodded toward Amigo, who was watching the humans with every appearance of curiosity and interest. "You have brought him along very well, I see—except perhaps for the water jumps," and he glanced with a knowing smile at her dripping condition. "There is a strand of weed above your left eye," he added kindly.

Blushing, Chloe made haste to wipe her forehead. "It is not his fault! I suddenly took thought that I had not schooled him to water jumps, and most foolishly lost my seat. He handled the jump like an expert—did you not, my friend?" she held out her hand to the stallion, who minced over and blew lovingly at her wet shirtfront, and then dropped his great head with an exaggerated sigh upon her shoulder. The sight of the small girl comforting the giant animal amused the watching men. Chloe was quick to note their smiles.

"You see, Milord, Amigo has a great sense of humor. Instead of souring or maddening him, his tribulations seem to have induced in him a sense of the comic in life—"

"As long as he is on the giving end of the jest," finished Rod. "He has a particular trick he is fond of playing upon my stableboys. With every appearance of cooperation, he raises his head just a little beyond their reach when they try to bridle him. I watched it one morning. Tom tried to reach him without success, then got a stool and tried again, but each time Amigo would raise his head just a little beyond Tom's reach. I had to put stop to it, in the interest of Tom's sanity." Then, catching a worried look from Milord, Rod reassured him. "There's no malice in him, I'd swear to that. And he belongs to Chloe, body and spirit. She can do anything with him."

"Except stay on his back at a water jump," added Milord wryly.

"Unfair! Unfair!" cried Chloe, on her mettle. "Just watch!" and mounting Amigo, she whirled him and set him cantering to the side of the field, where she opened the gate and took him back to the other side of the hedge. There she set the great stallion once more at the hedge, and he soared over it easily, and came cantering

100

toward them with the small triumphant figure waving from his back.

Lord Randal said, smiling, "I do not know why it should be amusing, for her horsemanship is excellent, and the horse is a marvel. But she's so *tiny*—"

"She is a great-heart," said Rod quietly. "I would hope that your lordship has only good in mind for her." His eyes met Lord Randal's in a level stare of challenge.

"Be assured of that," retorted Milord crisply. Then, as he returned the other's searching glance, he added, "You are a most unusual—lout, sir."

"I am probably better educated than your lordship," said Rod. "And I am certainly bigger. Perhaps we may someday put our respective—er—talents to the test?"

"I shall look forward to it," agreed Lord Randal, smiling a trifle grimly.

"*After* I have persuaded Miss Keith to marry me," continued Rod. "I don't wish to place any impediments in the path of that."

"And you think I might present an impediment?" enquired Milord with interest.

"Let us say that Miss Keith has a kind and loyal heart, that she thinks herself under some obligation to your lordship, and that I would not wish to render you incapacitated before I had secured her pledge to myself," explained Rod with a smooth insolence quite equal to Milord's.

The latter stared at him for a long moment; then he smiled with real enjoyment. "May I say that I am very pleased to have made your acquaintance, Mr. McLeod?" he said as he extended his hand.

The giant clasped it firmly in his great fist.

Lord Randal returned the crushing grip. "And you don't need to warn me that you could pull me out of the saddle with a single heave!"

101

"I would sooner land a tiger on my chest," Rod admitted.

"A tiger? Or a Tiger?" mocked Milord.

"At this moment, either," said Rod with a grin.

"Now *you* put me in mind of a lion," said Lord Randal.

"I take that kindly," Rod answered. "Most people call me an elephant."

Just then Chloe dismounted beside them, glancing a little anxiously at the two men. They seemed to be friendly enough, conversing about animals.

"Are you talking of the Tower Zoo in London?" she asked.

"No, but I came to talk about something similar," said Lord Randal. "There is a fine trick rider, one Sergeant-Major Philip Astley, who has a school and riding ring in a field near Westminster Bridge. He's prospered, but more because of his exhibitions of riding than from his school. I thought perhaps you might wish to come to London with me to see a performance." He glanced at Rod. "It might give you some ideas," he added with a provocative smile.

Rod intervened smoothly. "Thank you, Milord! An excellent thought! I'll take Miss Keith to London shortly. Is the performance staged every day?"

"I have tickets for you," Lord Randal produced them from a pocket in his modish riding coat. "The structure is roofed, so one can be comfortable even in inclement weather. And if you should wish to have a horse broken, or trained, Mr. Astley will do it for you and then tell you how he did it—for half a guinea!"

Chloe's eyes were beginning to sparkle. "What else does he do?"

"His special trick has been to ride with one foot on the horse's saddle and the other on his head, while brandishing a sword in the air. Of late he has taken to galloping upside down, with his head resting, not on the saddle, but on a pint-pot which is set on the saddle!"

"Is it a trick?" breathed Chloe.

"No," Milord answered seriously. "He is a brave man and a superb rider but he is more than that. He discovered that when a horse is ridden quickly *in a circle,* centrifugal force, that power which tends to make you move away from the center when you are going around in a circle, can help you to stay upright even on a moving surface like a horse's back." He paused, intent on the girl's vivid, enthralled expression.

"Yes, I see it!" she whispered. "You would *lean into* the force, resisting it, and it would hold you up!" She laughed in triumph. "I see!"

"I am glad," said Lord Randal politely. "I hope you will enjoy the performance. There are several ladies riding, also. It is entertaining to watch."

"We shall come tomorrow, shall we not, Rod? Can we get away?"

Rod sighed and quirked an eyebrow at Lord Randal. "Oh, I think it can be arranged. With Matt to direct them, Sam and Tom can take over the heavy duties for one day. Why don't you ride back quickly and consult with Aunt Janet? Perhaps she would like to see the show also."

"Oh, yes!" agreed Chloe. She turned to smile dazzlingly at Lord Randal. "How good you are to come all this way to give us a treat! Thank you, Milord."

She mounted Amigo and galloped off, a small rider on the huge steed, both of them obviously exulting in the joy of untrammeled movement. The men watched her go. Then Rod said,

"Was that why you came, Milord? To give us pleasure?"

"I am damned if I know," admitted his lordship. "But I rather think it was because I could not stay away."

"She is not of your world. You can bring her only sorrow," Rod said sternly.

"You think I would do that?" challenged Beresford.

"Not deliberately, no. But what can there be between you?"

Milord did not answer, but stared after the girl and the horse with eyes which did not see the green fields and the smokey towers and roofs of London in the distance. After a time, he turned his roan and rode off without another word.

Chapter Nine

THE PARTY LEFT Kindlewick Farm very early the next morning.

Aunt Janet was unexpectedly elegant in a plain brown traveling dress with a cape to match. Chloe had found a similar costume laid out in her bedroom when she retired the evening before. By candlelight, it appeared almost purple, but when the girl put it on in the morning, she saw how well the rich color, a deep vibrant red, suited her tanned face and dark curls. Aunt Janet had also provided a small straw hat with a dashing, upturned brim, bound with velvet ribbon to match the dress.

Appearing in the new garment at breakfast, Chloe found her throat closing as she tried to express her gratitude. "It is the prettiest dress I have ever had," she began. Aunt Janet hugged her and seated her at the table.

"Hush, child! It gave me pleasure to make it for you.

And it suits your coloring even better than I expected. Come along, now, we must eat breakfast quickly, lest Rod go on without us! He's been up for hours, superintending the departure of the wagons to market."

Feeling far too happy to eat, Chloe forced down some porridge and oatcakes at Janet's insistence. They came out onto the front steps just as Rod drove his vehicle around from the stables. Instead of the humble gig she had expected, Chloe beheld, with a gasp of pleasure, a phaeton painted lustrous mahogany, the wheels picked out in gold, the folding top neatly laid back. Rod was driving two powerful bay horses, whose shining hides matched the glossy phaeton. Perched beside his master sat young Alan, the second groom, in impeccable livery of brown and fawn. The lad jumped down at once to help the ladies into the rear seat and spread a rug over their knees.

"Handsome turnout, isn't it?" asked Janet complacently.

"Oh, yes!" breathed Chloe, but her eyes were all for Rod, quietly resplendent in a coat of sherry brown with brass buttons, and a dark plaid kilt. At his throat a plain white stock covered the strong column of his throat. A Glengarry bonnet, sporting an eagle feather, rode on his curly hair. To the girl's eyes, he was every inch a romantic Highlander, much more impressive than the teasing man in the homespun and high boots she saw daily around the farm.

When the ladies were settled in the rear seat, Rod set his pair in motion, and the phaeton moved smartly down the lane and onto the highroad. Aunt Janet discoursed on points of interest as they approached London, but Chloe found her attention wandering back to the broad shoulders and curly golden hair of the man in front of her.

The drive through London was exciting, but left her

feeling confused by the multiplicity of sights and sounds and smells. There was too much to see. Chloe began to realize, as they passed through the poorer districts, how fortunate she was to have found the safe haven of Kindlewick.

At length they crossed Westminster Bridge. At the south end, they beheld an heroic figure. In full military uniform, riding a white charger and brandishing a sword, Sergeant-Major Philip Astley touted the show at his newly-named Royal Grove. Starting as the British Riding School in a roped-off piece of open ground, Astley's venture had grown by this time to an imposing, completely roofed-over, two-story building. Its name had been changed twice, and it was now the Royal Grove, although most Londoners still called it Astley's Amphitheater.

Rod pulled up beyond the building in a field full of vehicles, and handed his aunt and Chloe out of the phaeton. Leaving Alan to mount guard over the equipage, Rod ushered the ladies into the Royal Grove. Chloe's eyes were even larger than usual as she stared around her avidly, absorbing every detail of the amazing building: the huge center ring, the stands and galleries which, Rod told her, seated three thousand persons, and which seemed to Chloe to be filled with chattering, colorful, elegant men and women who looked and sounded like a giant cageful of parrots.

When they were finally seated, under a ceiling painted with foliage, Chloe found a great deal to observe although the performance had not yet begun. She stole several long glances around, in an effort to discover whether Milord Beresford might be present. At the end of one of these reconnaissances, she met Rod's quizzical gaze and dropped her own glance, blushing. He made no comment, for which she was grateful.

Then the show began. She forgot everything in the

wonder of the horses. Their beauty and expertise held her entranced. There was much more than trick riding, although that in itself was almost unbelievable. Some of the acts did not even use horses, but to Chloe, even the hilarious clowns, the fabulous acrobats, and the artist who walked upon a thin rope high above the ground, were not as fascinating as the glorious, shining horses, with their clever narrow heads, huge shining eyes, and skillful hooves. How she envied the men—and women!—who performed upon these beautiful animals as though both horses and riders had wings! Mrs. Astley rode two horses at once, balancing upon those great moving backs as gently and steadily as though she walked upon the safe earth. The highlight of the day's performance, aside of course from the much advertised sight of Philip Astley riding upside down with his head on a pint-pot, was the tumbling skill of one James Lawrence, who was dressed as the Devil and, from a trampoline, threw a somersault over twelve horses! Chloe hardly had time to breathe, so fast and furiously did wonder pile upon wonder. Rod watched her flushed, ecstatic little face with an expression which Aunt Janet, catching a look at it, could not quite decipher.

But there were others who looked also. At the end of the show, when Rod was leading the dazzled girl out of the amphitheater by one arm, a well-known voice hailed them.

Coming toward them was Milord Randal, with a strikingly lovely young woman on his arm. Chloe thought she had never seen anything daintier than the mass of shining red curls that peeped out from under a modish ostrich-plumed bonnet, the black-lashed green eyes, and the delicate features of his lordship's companion.

"Lady Barbara, may I present Miss McLeod, Miss

Keith, and Mr. McLeod?" He turned to the Kindlewick party. "My cousin, Lady Barbara Dickson."

While the women were nodding and saying all the proper things, Lord Randal shook hands with Rod. "She liked it?"

"I feared for awhile she'd be over the railing and into the arena," confessed Rod. "I only hope she will not feel called upon to emulate Lawrence and leap over every horse in my stables!"

"She's a delightful child," agreed Lord Randal.

Rod gave him a long glance. "Not a child," he said softly. "But she is determined. I pray you may not have started something I can't control."

Milord frowned. "You don't mean to say that the girl may set up her *own*—"

"Or seek to join this one," said Rod.

"Surely not?"

"Not if I can help it," agreed Rod in the firmest voice Janet, who was shamelessly eavesdropping, had ever heard him use. She smiled a secret smile. Then she turned to Chloe, who was in eager discussion with Milord's beautiful companion over the merits of the various acts.

"I think we must be going now," she said, quietly. "We have rather a tiring drive back to Kindlewick Farm."

But Chloe was not to escape without a final confrontation. As the two parties moved slowly out to the field where the various vehicles were waiting, a loud voice sounded just behind her.

"Lady Barbara! Your servant! And my *dear* friend Beresford!"

Again Chloe felt the sudden icy chill which she had experienced at the Robbins's inn. She did not turn to look at the man who spoke, but increased her pace toward the brown phaeton Alan was trying to bring

109

through the jostling mass to them. Rod and Janet, aware of her pallid face, moved quickly after her. Lord Randal was too busy seeking to fend off Sir Jerold from his cousin to notice their departure. Rod lifted the ladies up into the phaeton, and leaping in, took the reins from Alan and began to move quickly through the press of vehicles to the road. He might have succeeded in getting the party away without attracting Sir Jerold's notice, had it not been for the efforts of Lady Barbara to wave a courteous good-bye to her new acquaintances. As she did so, calling Lord Randal's attention to the departure, Sir Jerold looked up also, and his eyes met Chloe's anxious ones. Although she averted her face at once, Peke stood momentarily frozen at attention. The last they saw of him, he was smiling a little as he turned again to address Lady Barbara.

They were across the bridge and moving north through London before anyone spoke. Then Rod said, "Who was that man who frightened you, Chloe?"

"It was Sir Jerold Peke," whispered the girl.

"The villain who struck Chloe in the face at the inn," supplied Janet. "While she was acting as Lord Randal's tiger."

Rod was looking grim. "I almost wish I had known it when he was within my reach," he muttered. "Do you think he recognized you, love?"

The unexpected use of the endearment quite overthrew Chloe's hard-held poise. She began to cry soundlessly. Aunt Janet took her in her arms. After a minute, the girl squared her shoulders. "I apologize for being such a watering-pot," she tried to make light of her anxiety. "But that man Peke is—is *evil!*"

"He has seen that you are under my protection and Aunt Janet's chaperonage," Rod pointed out calmly. "There is nothing he can do to harm you now. And I

110

wager he will think twice before trying to seek you out at the farm."

Chloe agreed hastily, not wanting to ruin the day's pleasure with her fears and alarms. She began to chat with real interest about the wonders they had seen, and joined in Aunt Janet's heartfelt expression of satisfaction when Rod disclosed that he had made a reservation for dinner for all of them at a quiet hotel on the north side of London. Chloe was impressed by the way in which Rod was treated—as though he were the laird of a powerful clan—and his party given the best table in the dining room.

"What is the name of this hotel?" she asked, shyly, after Rod had ordered the meal for them.

"McLeod's," the big man said with a chuckle. Then, at her startled glance, "No, I do not own it. But the owner is one of my best customers—and we Highlanders band together in Sassenach territory."

While they were eating, Chloe told herself that her fear of Sir Jerold was irrational, for what, she asked herself, could he *do* when Milord was forewarned and ready? After coming to this comfortable decision, the girl turned to Aunt Janet and said brightly, "What a beautiful girl Lord Randal's cousin is, is she not? And so conversable!"

"A regular pocket Venus," agreed Rod, with what Chloe felt was rather too much warmth. "Those curls—those green eyes—!"

"And that bonnet with the ostrich plumes!" added Janet, in such an envious voice that both the young people were betrayed into a laugh.

The rest of the dinner went on very lightheartedly, and Chloe felt, as she was being helped back into Rod's phaeton in the dusk, that she had never enjoyed a day more in her life. Even Alan, full to repletion from the dinner he had been served in the hotel kitchen, was

111

quite prepared for the moonlight journey back to the farm, although he kept falling asleep and having to be rescued from a tumble into the road every half hour. They completed the journey in good time; the horses were mettlesome and eager to step out for home; the road shone white in the moonlight. Chloe thought she had never known such deep content, and drifted off to sleep herself, with her eyes on the broad shoulders before her.

At dinner in Milord Dickson's elegant town house, Lady Barbara was talking about Mr. Roderick McLeod. "He was overwhelming, Papa," she told her amused and indulgent father. "At least *seven* feet tall, and his shoulders as broad as a *door!* Randal will bear me out—he was wearing a *skirt!* Although I vow I've never beheld a more *manly* man in my life!"

Her father laughed, but Lord Randal's grin was a trifle forced. "He's an unregenerate Highlander, sir, but I must admit I've never seen him in a kilt before. Owns a prosperous market-farm outside the city."

"A *farmer?*" asked Barbara and her father in unison. Then the girl laughed. "He *couldn't* be!"

"My word on it," answered Randal lazily. "Take you out there one day to see the fellow in all his—uh—bucolic glory," he offered.

"For Gad's sake don't call his kilt a skirt," advised her father. "The rebellious savages were forbidden by law to wear 'em for years after their defeat at Culloden Moor."

"I can't imagine anyone *forbidding* Mr. McLeod to do anything," murmured Barbara, with a provocative glance at her cousin.

His answering smile was wary. "Don't tell me I shall

112

have to be fending off Rod McLeod, Barbara! As if I had not enough trouble with Sir Jerold!"

"Is that fortune hunter still hanging about?" growled Lord Dickson. "I told you, Barbara, if *you* cannot discourage him, *I'll* send him to the right-about!"

"He is a *toad*," said the girl succinctly. "As for Rod McLeod, Randal, I don't think you'll have to act the dragon where *he* is concerned. I suspect his eyes are turned in quite another direction." Smiling a little at Lord Randal's disconcerted expression, she went on softly, "Yes, I fancy our braw Highlander has his eyes on little Miss Keith—the *lucky* girl!"

Lord Randal discovered that, for some reason he did not understand, that idea displeased him.

By the time Sir Jerold Peke had located his groom, mounted his horse, fought his way through the undisciplined crowds streaming away from the Royal Grove, and set off after the brown and gold phaeton, it was already too late. After a fruitless half-hour search he was forced to admit that he had lost it. He gave up, and returned to his lodgings in Clarges Street in bad temper. Over several glasses of brandy, he considered the startling possibilities which the encounter at Astley's had suggested to him. If the girl in the dark-red dress was indeed the same person as the grubby tiger who had been in attendance on Beresford at that inn, then Jerold Peke had within his grasp a chance to get revenge on a man he hated.

If only he had not lost sight of the brown phaeton! It was a prime turnout, the horses better than anything he himself had ever owned. Could he have been mistaken? He bit his knuckles, a prey to indecision and fear. Beresford and his cousin had been talking to the girl and her companions. If Peke's suspicions were correct, and the chit really had been masquerading as a boy in Lord Randal's company, would he have dared to flaunt her before the Lady Barbara? It seemed wildly unlikely.

On the other hand, Peke thought he could not have been mistaken in those huge gray eyes. And the girl *had* recognized him! There had been shock and fear in her gaze. Peke recalled with enjoyment the moment when his fist had hit the Tiger's jaw—the satisfying contact with vulnerable flesh and fragile bone. No, he could not be mistaken! The girl was the same creature who had been sharing Lord Randal's room at the inn.

Pouring himself another glass of brandy, Sir Jerold began to consider how best he might use this damning information against Beresford. Order Peke away from the Lady Barbara, would he? Well, perhaps Sir Jerold would do some ordering of his own! Still, best not to hurry. There could be more than one kind of profit to be got from this situation! Sir Jerold began to smile gloatingly as he drained his glass and made his plans.

Chapter Ten

CHLOE COULD HARDLY WAIT to get out to the stables the following morning. As she fed and groomed Molly and Amigo, she told the stallion about the fascinating show she had seen at the Royal Grove.

"They were not so beautiful as you, my friend," she concluded, "but they had the advantage of better training than I have known how to give." She sighed wistfully. "If I could only have taken you with me, to see them—" She paused, much struck by the idea. Then she finished softly, stroking his warm, soft nose, "If you had seen them, you could have imitated what they did, given half a chance!"

Amigo regarded her coquettishly with one lovely large dark eye. The girl chuckled. "Yes, I know what a wag you are! 'Imitate them?' you are saying! 'Given half a chance I could improve upon anything they can do!'—and the devil of it is, I believe you! So now we must plan how we can get you in to watch the lovely horses at the Royal Grove. But first, I think, we'll try what I can do to teach you some of their tricks, shall we?"

Amigo was delighted at the idea, and pawed eagerly, snorting and blowing, until Chloe had him bridled and on their way to the furthest paddock. For the girl was not going to risk premature discovery of her plans for the stallion. She had a pretty good idea that Rod's canny view of the situation would focus clearly upon conscientious work with her new students, and look askance at any harebrained, foolhardy schemes for making a trick horse out of Amigo.

The first of the students were to come out from London this afternoon. Everything was ready at the stables. She had, therefore, the morning free if she wished to show Amigo some tricks. Rod was usually busy overseeing the work of his young farmers at this time; the grooms were exercising Rod's horses in the paddocks nearer the farmhouse. Even Aunt Janet was occupied with the accounts today. The coast should be clear.

Chloe rode the stallion out to the furthest paddock. He took his time, running through his paces with precision and a tremendous complacency. Chloe chuckled.

"You really are a conceited fellow, you know," she chided him. "A regular coxcomb—a saucy peacock!"

Amigo preened himself, frisking and bounding in a series of curvets as he heard the beloved voice. The pleasant music of the girl's laughter rang across the fields as the two friends proceeded in perfect harmony to the lesson.

At first all went well. Chloe knew a great deal about horses, whatever her lack of knowledge of fancy show-tricks. She understood the wonderful memory of the horse, his curiosity about new things, his sense of fun. She also understood how to work with him, making every step of a new routine clear, and not confusing him with hard new physical challenges until he had mastered the earlier ones. Today she planned only to give Amigo some idea of the fun in store. Reaching her chosen field, she began to trot, then canter, then gallop. Amigo entered into the exercise eagerly. She directed his motion in a huge circle, and found that, as always, the horse responded flawlessly to her signals of hand and leg.

"And now, my friend," the girl slid to the ground and took off Amigo's saddle and her own riding boots, "let us see whether we shall shine as an equestrian team." She remounted, and set the stallion to galloping around in a wide circle again. Then, with a little quiver of excitement, she balanced her body and got slowly to her knees.

Amigo's ears flicked back and forward. He was not especially apprehensive; he had decided that his little human was his friend, and would not hurt him. Still, her behavior was peculiar, to say the least. She was moving around on his back in a very odd manner. Was she ill? Did it behoove him, as the male leader of the herd, to protect her? He shook his head against the reins and whickered inquiringly.

Chloe, holding her breath, got slowly to her feet and stood upright, her toes curling in an unconscious gripping action. For one glorious instant she stood tall, moving gracefully to the sway of the galloping horse. And then Amigo, worried by this unaccustomed behavior, stopped short and looked around at his rider. Who promptly lost her balance and fell to the ground.

Picking herself up gingerly, Chloe heard startled laughter. She turned to face Rod, seated on his big gray, an amused audience of one at her first, less than successful performance as a trick rider.

As she watched him, he stopped laughing and said

117

mockingly, "You did say his talent was for comedy," he grinned.

Chloe did not know whether she was more embarrassed or angry. While she was trying to decide between two cutting retorts, Rod spoke again, and this time there was no trace of amusement in his voice.

"You, of all people, should know that it takes *time!* Time and patience. And what if you are hurt? You cannot run your school if you cripple yourself! Nor do you present the correct image to the parents of the students I secured for you, indulging in trick riding and dangerous circus buffoonery! Carnival fare, Miss Keith—not professional behavior!"

The big man seemed to be whipping himself up into a rage, his voice becoming louder and harsher as he finished, "I had thought you had a more dignified goal in mind!"

Stunned by the bitterness of his attack, Chloe tried at first to make light of the situation. "I don't intend to fall often, Rod. And I do, very much, want to teach the students you found for me." At his sardonic expression, the girl began to bristle. "I can teach my students and still have time to train Amigo in a few simple tricks—" she protested.

"I know your 'few simple tricks'!" sneered Rod. "The next thing any of us know, you'll be off to London hanging about Astley's with the other clowns!"

As soon as he said it, Rod knew he had done the unforgivable. Gray-faced, Chloe began to saddle up Amigo. Then she put her boots back on, mounted, and cantered off to the stables without uttering another word. Rod stared moodily after her, unable during those crucial moments to think of a placating phrase which might have assuaged the hurt he had dealt her. He still believed he was correct in his attitude; perhaps it was better to be harsh now, before Chloe's enthusiasm got out of control; better to nip the folly before the child got too far involved in some harebrained scheme. Still, he admitted to himself morosely, he would rather not have brought that look of shocked dismay to the girl's face—to say nothing of the hard frozen expression with which she had ridden away from him.

It did not please him at all to learn, that evening, from Aunt Janet, that Chloe had discussed with her the possibility of the girl riding Amigo to London one day the following week. Chloe had already gone quietly to bed, and the two McLeods were seated in front of the fire, idly discussing plans for next season, when Aunt Janet asked Rod if he knew of Chloe's latest start, and upon his rather wary inquiry, disclosed it.

"I hope you discouraged her," Rod snapped, sitting upright and glaring in his aunt's direction.

She raised a quizzical eyebrow. "Here's heat! Am I to infer that you have talked of her schemes with the girl already?"

"I have forbidden her to waste any time on these circus tricks!" Rod retorted. "If that damn fool Beresford had minded his own business, we should not be faced with this dangerous folly. He knew the girl was horse-mad! Taking her to Astley's! An idiot could have guessed how she would react!"

"Then why didn't you?" challenged Janet outrageously. "I seem to remember you jockeying Lord Beresford out of the opportunity of taking her so you could bestow the treat upon her yourself."

"The more fool I," groaned Rod. "She'll kill herself trying to emulate the trained equestriennes—or cripple herself—or ruin the horse—"

"To say nothing of leaving Kindlewick Farm," finished Janet. "She may become the rage of London.

119

She's brave enough, and I do believe she has special gifts with animals."

Rod had apparently heard nothing after the first of his aunt's speech, for his face had set into a grimace of disapproval. "'The rage of London'!" he quoted with disgust. "The object of the distasteful attentions of every jacked-up demi-beau and mushroom in the metropolis! Is that what you wish for your old friend's daughter?"

"Of course not," Janet replied. "Nor do I think she will accept such unpleasant attentions, or even be aware of them, for the most part. She is a particularly innocent girl for her years, and not what I believe you call 'approachable'—"

Roderick rejected with every mark of revulsion the idea that he would use such a term about any young woman. "It is all these whelps of noble houses whom you have been obliged to instruct," he said darkly. "You have picked up some pretty highly-seasoned language."

Aunt Janet laughed at him. "And you, my dear nephew, are like a bear nursing a sore paw. What has set you all on end? I take it that you have quarreled with the girl—hurt her pretty badly, I would say, from the look and sound of her tonight at dinner. Why must you be at dagger-drawing with her, Rod? I thought you were beginning to like her a little?"

"Like her!" snapped her nephew. "I'd as soon take a tiger to my bosom!"

Aunt Janet broke into a hearty laugh. "Well, my language may be highly-seasoned, but yours, I take leave to inform you, is shabby-genteel! Your *bosom,* indeed!"

"Well, to my bed, then, if we are to adopt your vocabulary." Rod's eyes were glittering with anger, his aunt noted with interest. She had seldom seen him in one of the notorious McLeod rages, but there was no doubt he was in one now. Chloe must really have hit upon a nerve. Janet wondered what they had quarreled about. On the whole, she was not displeased. Better open antagonism than polite boredom.

"I wonder what brought that particular metaphor to your mind?" she asked him, and chuckled at the look of loathing which followed the flash of awareness in his face.

"What exactly is your objection to her riding to London one day—aside of course from the fear that she might be molested? And we should send a groom with her to prevent any such disagreeable incident."

"One: she might be seriously injured trying those tricks," gritted Rod. "Two: if she were hurt, or even if she spent too much time at Astley's, she would lose the good students I have secured for her. And I *thought*," he concluded with awful irony, "that her whole purpose in coming here—as well as yours in bringing her—was to help her to establish her riding school." Then, as if unable to endure the conversation longer, Rod got up and, with chilling courtesy, bid his aunt a very good night.

The next few days passed without untoward incident. The two principals treated one another with a politeness so frigid it was insulting. This behavior did not worry Janet as much as the look in Chloe's eyes. The child was not happy, in spite of the remarkable success of her first teaching efforts. The parents who accompanied their children to the first few lessons had been united and generous in their praise of the new riding school and the young woman who was its instructor. They assumed that Rod McLeod himself was the director, and had left messages of approval of Miss Keith with the head groom, whom Rod had ordered to assist Chloe in any way possible. Rod had intended that role for himself the first few days, telling himself he should stand by to help the chit if she lost her head. However, after their very unpleasant encounter in the far field the morning before the first lesson, he had kept himself out of the way. He had allowed himself to anticipate a reconciliation—surely the girl would realize that he had had only her own good in mind when he spoke to her so sharply after her fall? He had in fact permitted his imagination to picture the details of their reconciliation: his own kindly forbearance, his quick and generous forgiveness of her defiance, when she retracted it, the warmth and sweetness of their new understanding—! At this point in his meditations, Rod found it necessary to saddle the gray and ride hard for half an hour.

In the event, however, their next conversation was not concerned with reconciliation. As they were rising from the dining table on Sunday, Chloe asked stiffly if Rod would be so good as to give her a few minutes in his office. Rod was understood to say it would be a pleasure. The young couple retired to the room in which the business of the farm was efficiently conducted by Mr. McLeod, and that gentleman offered Miss Keith a chair with all the kindly forbearance he had imagined.

Chloe sat down and raised her great anxious eyes to meet his. "Now," he thought, with a stirring of his senses, "she will tell me she regrets our quarrel and her part in it . . ."

Unfortunately, the girl's first words were, "I'm going to do it, you know. I am aware you do not like it above half; in fact, for some reason I cannot fathom, you are thrown into a rage at the idea. However," and she drew a deep breath, "I would like to tell you that I am riding Amigo into London tomorrow morning, to see if I can talk to Mr. and Mrs. Astley. I shall of course return

122

early tomorrow evening, so that I shall be fresh and rested for the lessons I must give on Tuesday."

"I intended to inform you, Miss Keith," said Rod with icy disapproval, "that I have arranged for two new students to attend tomorrow afternoon. Sir Peter Daley—a friend of Lord Beresford's—is bringing his young brother and sister out for their first lesson."

Chloe gasped and tried to read the impassive countenance. "But that is wonderful! I could wish that you had told me about this a little sooner—but I shall try to be back in good time for their lesson. When do they arrive?"

"Lord Peter said he would get them here at three o'clock. Do you think perhaps you might postpone your little jaunt to the circus until a day when you have no responsibilities to your students?"

Chloe had almost decided that she would do just that, but something about Rod's manner was so abrasive that she felt all her anger and hurt rising in a hot tide to her throat. So strong was her reaction that she felt almost ill. Drawing a deep breath, she stood up and faced the man.

"I shall have to leave very early, then, to get back in time, shall I not?" her voice sounded brittle in her own ears.

"After what I have just said, you still intend to go?" The angry glitter which Janet had noticed in his eyes was there again.

"I do," replied Chloe firmly.

"Then I must warn you that if you are not here to instruct Sir Peter's brother and sister, we must think about the possibility that Kindlewick Farm is not the place for your efforts. I," Rod concluded, with a lamentable descent from the high tone he had taken, "resent being made a fool of by a girl who doesn't care enough about her school to attend to her students."

123

The note of drama he had thought to inject into the interview became farce when both participants, blazingly angry, turned at the same moment to make a dignified exit from the room and collided at the door. It was hard to tell who came off worse from the unexpected encounter. Chloe had the breath knocked out of her by the impact with his huge, powerful body, though it struck her only a glancing, unintentional blow. However, her evil genius, ever aware of the ludicrous, forced a laugh from her. At the sound of which Rod drew back with a hiss of rage and held the door for her. Chloe scuttled through and ran up to her room.

Chapter Eleven

CHLOE HAD NOT IMAGINED that her second trip to Astley's Royal Grove would begin so miserably. She arose very early, well before the dawn, dressed, and crept down the stairs and out to the stables without disclosing her presence to anyone. There was a light in the kitchen, but fearful lest it be Rod, rising early to superintend the setting off of the market wagons, she did not stop to break her fast.

The smaller stable in which Amigo had his stall was empty of people, but a lantern burned, giving enough light for her to saddle and bridle her horse. Within minutes she was on her way toward the highroad. She was pretty sure she could find the proper route, and she did get herself to the outskirts of London in good time. However, for the last ten minutes or so she had been sure she heard horse's hooves behind her. It came to her, not without a pleasant surge of angry anticipation, that the follower might be the abominable Mr.

McLeod. She drew to the side of the road and waited for her pursuer to catch up. There was traffic upon the London road, but not enough to conceal the identity of the man who came after her. To her surprise, it was young Alan, mounted upon a pretty little mare.

She greeted him with welcome tinged with suspicion.

"It's my day off," said the youth with every appearance of pleasure. "I thought I'd look around London a bit, and maybe get to see that Astley's place. I never did get to go in, you know. I had to mind the horses!"

At once Chloe's soft heart was wrung. It was true, the boy had stayed with the phaeton while the rest of the party were inside enjoying the performance. "It is beyond anything great," she said, encouragingly. "Perhaps we might go together? That is where I am bound, also, but I am not just completely sure I have got the way clear in my mind."

Since this was exactly why Rod had sent Alan after her, but with strict injunctions not to admit it to her, Alan was quite agreeable to joining forces with Miss Keith. So they proceeded in great charity with one another, and a fascinated and rather fearful joy in the wonders and terrors of the great city.

Chloe had dressed in the new riding habit Aunt Janet had had made for her in the male style without a skirt, for convenience in teaching, and had placed a cap over her curls, so that to the casual eye they looked like two lads off for an outing in the great city. The more knowledgeable viewer might have wondered a little at the quality of the horses they rode, but at this early hour there were few such to note them. In less time than Chloe had anticipated, they crossed Westminster Bridge and turned down toward the Royal Grove. Early though it was, there was activity about the large building. They rode around to the rear of the building and, meeting a kindly-looking man, they informed him they had come to see the wonderful show, and Chloe added that she would wish to speak to either Mr. or Mrs. Astley about getting a job.

It was not so much their appearance as the undeniable breeding of their handsome horses which won a reluctant permission from the guardian of the building. Within a few minutes the two mounts were placed in an enclosure with some of the Astley horses, and Chloe and Alan followed their guide into the Royal Grove.

Mrs. Astley, a heavy, rather loud-voiced woman, greeted them pleasantly enough. Young Alan hardly answered her, so taken by the fascination of the scene was he. He stared around open-mouthed, as though not knowing where to look next. The huge building was alive with activity. Riders dressed in odd grubby garments worked with their fabulous horses, acrobats ran through their act, clowns rehearsed their tumbles and far above the ground on a tight rope, a slender man ran back and forth as calmly as though he were on the firm cobblestones of the city. As he scanned this kaleidoscope of activity, Alan's glance fell upon two young women who stood beside a handsome stallion. Suddenly magnetized, the youth walked over toward them.

Chloe, meanwhile, was introducing herself to Mrs. Astley, who seemed a good-hearted woman for all her brusque manner.

"My name is Keith," the girl began. "I have a small riding school just north of London, at Kindlewick Farm. I own a thoroughbred stallion who can be trained, I believe, as you have trained your wonderful horses. I— I had hopes that you might show me how to do it?"

"Lord love you, girl, it ain't that simple!" laughed the woman. "Takes years of practice to bring 'em to what

127

you see here. How old are you? And how old's the horse?"

"I am twenty-one," Chloe confessed. "Amigo is about three."

Mrs. Astley shook her head regretfully. "Too old, me dear. Both of you."

"But surely—if I came once a week, there would be much I could learn?"

The older woman looked at her carefully, assessing her ability and determination. What she saw in the small dedicated face seemed to impress her, but she said slowly, "It's more than what you want to do or can do. There's the horse to be considered. Not all of 'em have the talent nor the sense to understand what's wanted."

Chloe's face brightened. "Amigo has! He's clever, and wise, and a great showoff! I rode him here today—if you'd just take a look at him?"

"You've brought him? That's good. I'll take a look, although the Sergeant-Major is the one who knows what's what. Astley can tell you in ten minutes whether or not a horse can be taught the routines." She smiled at the anxious girl. "Maybe—just *maybe*, mind!—if you was to get a room nearby, come in every day and work hard, then in three or four months we'd see. But it depends on the horse, as I've told you."

Chloe shook her head. "I couldn't leave my school. I'm just getting it started, and it's my living."

Mrs. Astley shrugged. "Well, then, dear, there's no more to be said. Look around the building—it's Astley's pride and joy—and you're welcome to stay and watch a performance, if you'd like."

"Won't you just look at Amigo while he's here?" pleaded the girl.

"Oh, very well, trot him out, dear," Mrs. Astley said good-naturedly. "Bring him into the ring."

Chloe felt, as she hurried out to the horse enclosure,

that the older woman was more than ready to get back to her own concerns, and was grateful for her forbearance. But when, a few minutes later, she rode Amigo into the ring, she occasioned a great deal of interest from the members of the troupe as well as their employer's wife. They came to watch with the child-like curiosity of human beings everywhere.

The great black stallion, a little nervous of this new place with its unfamiliar sights, sounds and smells, was also intensely curious, and reassured by the presence of so many other horses. He pranced and curvetted and pawed at the ground, and sent out his clarion challenge, and seemed very conscious of his own virility and skill. Chloe pulled him up in front of Mrs. Astley, where, on command, he made his elegant bow to the good woman's hearty applause. She stepped forward, beaming, to stroke his neck. Amigo bowed his great head to her caress, accepting her admiration as his due.

"What a boyo he is! And doesn't he know it!" she chuckled, and moved forward to examine his points. She noticed his scars, and her face darkened as she shot a look of inquiry at the girl. Chloe anticipated her question.

"I rescued him from a brute who was trying to kill him. He's only just got back to trusting people."

Mrs. Astley stroked the strong, warm neck. "A real beauty, no mistake! What a pity he's so marred!"

"But he's clever, and funny," urged the girl. "The terrible treatment he received didn't sour him." She told the story of her rescue from the water jump, and his playful tricks with the grooms.

"So he's a comedian, is he?" Mrs. Astley looked thoughtful. "Maybe the Sergeant-Major should see him. He might work as a clown act with you."

Chloe was enthusiastic. "Oh, do you think Sergeant-Major Astley would be willing to take a look at Amigo?"

The girl had almost lost hope when Mrs. Astley had echoed Rod's opinion that proper training would require years of daily work. However, it might be possible that the Sergeant-Major would give her suggestions as to how she could work with Amigo in her spare time every day. She could manage that without interrupting her classes with the children. But there was a disappointment in store for her. It appeared that Sergeant-Major Astley had gone off to the city to buy fireworks for a gala performance, and it was not certain exactly when he would return.

"Why not wait and talk to him, dear?" urged Mrs. Astley. "There's lots you'd like to see, and plenty of food if you're hungry!"

When she consulted him, Alan was pleased to remain. He had struck up an acquaintance with several of the younger performers, and could imagine nothing more interesting than spending the day with them. As for Chloe, she received the invitation with gratitude, and accepted a spicy but satisfying plate of spaghetti cooked by the Italian mother of two of the acrobats.

There was so much to see and do that Chloe did not realize how rapidly the day was passing. She was flattered, too, by the attention Amigo aroused, and amused by his greedy acceptance of admiration. She was abruptly brought back to earth by a reluctant comment from young Alan.

"It'll be past suppertime before we gets home, Miss Chloe. Maybe we better not wait for the Sergeant-Major?"

Recalled to her obligations, shocked at her unthinking neglect, Chloe bid her kind hostess a hasty farewell and fled.

It was almost dark when Kindlewick Farm loomed

ahead of them. Lights were on in the farmhouse and in the stables. Chloe dismissed Alan, and he slipped thankfully off to the stables leading Amigo. Chloe hurried up to the front door and entered quietly. The big front hall was ablaze with lamps. As the girl closed the door softly behind her, a cold voice brought her sharply around.

"So you have decided to give us the pleasure of your company at last, Miss Keith?" Rod stood in the parlor doorway, seeming to fill the space with his huge, rigid frame. His eyes glittered with rage.

"We—I was delayed in London. It is not Alan's fault he was so long away. He stayed to be my escort."

"It is solely for that reason that I do not dismiss him out of hand," snapped Rod. "He showed no surprise that they had joined forces," thought Chloe, and the image entered her mind of herself and Alan, two children in a toy shop, forgetting everything but their own pleasure. Hastily she dismissed the picture, and began her explanation.

"I was waiting for Sergeant-Major Astley to return. His wife was kind enough to promise me he would grant me an interview when he got back to the Royal Grove."

Her inquisitor was relentless. "I believe I had informed you that I had arranged a private lesson for the younger Daleys at three, had I not?"

"You did," the girl agreed, her eyes steadfast on his, her color high.

"You agreed to return in time for the lesson," Rod continued. "Accepting your word in this matter, I allowed Sir Peter Daley to bring his young brother and sister here this afternoon. They waited nearly two hours before giving up and returning to London. The children were disappointed."

Chloe stared at his impassive face in which only the

angry eyes seemed alive. She could find nothing to say in her defense. She had indeed told him she would return in time, but in the excitement of Astley's she had forgotten completely. It was unbelievable—appalling. She bent her head. "I am at fault," she said miserably.

She did not catch the merest softening in Rod's expression, and his voice, when he spoke again, was still cold and hard with disapproval.

"Lord Beresford accompanied the party. It seems Sir Peter is his best friend. He had added his persuasions to mine that the children meet you, and possibly enroll as students in your classes." Ignoring the stricken look in the great eyes, he continued sarcastically, "It appears you are not so anxious to establish a riding school as you gave my aunt to believe. I have been thinking hard about your proposal, and I am afraid you have not convinced me that you are in earnest about this school. Running off to see a circus when you should be attending to your work—!"

Chloe, gray-faced under her tan, spoke at last. "I have admitted that my behavior today was irresponsible and rude," she said in a hoarse voice.

"It was indeed," Rod agreed grimly.

The girl's smile was pitiful. "I apologize to you, and I'll write to ask Sir Peter's pardon. And Lord Randal's, of course, although I think *he* might understand, having been with me when I found Amigo."

For some reason, Chloe's reference to Beresford seemed to add fresh fuel to Rod's anger. "Very fine," he sneered. "And the next time you decide you want to show off Amigo's tricks, we shall have you jauntering off to London without thought of those who must remain here and make excuses for you—!"

"You are too severe!" Chloe cried out. "I have accepted your chastisement—offered my apologies—!"

"But not," said Rod obstinately, "your word that you will not run off again. For what it's worth," he added, unforgivably.

Chloe searched the man's face for a long moment. He stared back at her without change of expression. The girl sighed—a short, unhappy exhalation which had in it something of acceptance. "I shall leave Kindlewick as soon as I can arrange for a room in the city," she said colorlessly.

Rod's eyebrows came together in a thunderous frown. "Running shy at the first blow?" he mocked. "Now we see how much your famous riding school meant to you!"

Chloe's head came up. "You cannot have it both ways, Mr. McLeod," she snapped back. "Either I am an embarrassing nuisance you wish to be rid of, or I am a human being who has made a mistake but will try to make amends! One thing I will not do is to remain here to be the whipping boy for your ill-humor!"

Rod raised his eyebrows. "Now it is my fault," he said angrily. "How very like a woman to wish to throw the blame for all her faults upon a man who—"

Aunt Janet, interrupting the quarrel at this very inopportune moment, came rushing out of the dining parlor. "A man who *what?*" Chloe wondered. But the moment was lost. Janet was glaring at her nephew.

"Are you ripping up at the child again, Roderick? Surely you are old enough to control your temper with the little lass?"

For some reason, this question pleased neither of her hearers. Janet eyed their vexed expressions sharply. Then she continued, "Will you be kind enough to tell me the cause of this latest brangle?"

Since neither of the two seemed anxious to speak, she went on, "It has to do with Chloe's absence from the

133

farm today, of course. I've already told you she had my permission to go—if such a ridiculous thing was necessary! She is not a prisoner, after all, but my guest."

Rod spoke as one at the uttermost limits of control. "Did she also have your permission to miss her meeting with two new students?" he snapped.

"I have said I will write an apology!" wailed Chloe. The various strains and excitements of this long day seemed to be catching up with her, and she had a disloyal wish that Aunt Janet had not come rushing to her aid at just this particular time. It was obvious that Rod was in a fine fury; his aunt's intervention seemed to have exacerbated his temper rather than soothing it.

Janet, who had become aware that she had interrupted at the wrong moment, said sharply, "You both seem to have made a great to-do over a very small matter. I had expected more maturity from you!"

This blighting comment did nothing to relieve the tension between the man and the girl. Janet observed their mutinous faces with the beginnings of satisfaction. Not indifferent to one another—oh, no! If ever they found their way past these initial rapids, the powerful flow of this much emotion would sweep them off their feet! The older woman sighed. Behind her slightly dictatorial manner lurked the soul of an incurable Romantic. It had long been her dream to make a match of it between these two young people.

Rod regained his composure first. With a formal little bow he offered his apology. "Pray forgive me, Miss Keith. Of course I have no right to influence you in any way. I bid you both good night!" and he swung out of the room like a Highland chieftain leaving a hostile clan, with his big shoulders squared and his back very straight.

Chloe felt desolated. Why did it have to be this way between them? All she wanted was to exist in reasonable amity with the man, wasn't it? She raised her glance to meet Janet's kindly regard. "Was it very bad, today—waiting for me to return?"

Janet smiled. "Not at all! Rod took the whole party through the stables, then mounted them on his best horses and conducted them on a tour around the property. The gentlemen were quite impressed. Then I served a collation, which, if I may make a pun, Chloe, went down very well with all of them. Rod brought out his best brandy for Milords." She paused. Should she confide in the girl her own suspicion that the root of Rod's anger came from his jealousy of Lord Randal? No, best not meddle with the situation. The young people must find their own way. Instead, she asked, "Have you eaten? One always feels better with a full stomach."

She led the way into the bright kitchen, where the kettle wheezed on the stove, and delectable smells filled the air. Chloe sat down and ate with a thankful heart. All she had eaten today was the plate of spicy spaghetti at the Royal Grove, and that had been hours ago. When she had finished the last crumb on the heaped plate Janet had given her, she sat back with a sigh of satisfaction. Janet poured her another cup of tea.

"It won't do, Aunt Janet," Chloe said reluctantly. "Rod is not happy to have me here."

"What about you? Are you happy at Kindlewick?" asked the older woman.

"Yes! It is above anything I had dared to hope! And you both have been more than kind. Rod has put himself out to be helpful, and I repay him with thoughtlessness, ingratitude—"

"Nonsense!" Janet said prosaically, restraining this flight of self-disparagement. "You didn't deliberately forget the new pupils, and they'll return next week, if

135

you wish them to! *Men!* They are forever putting everything at sixes and sevens with their childish starts! You must be patient with him, Chloe. He is really an excellent person—for a male."

Chloe laughed reluctantly. "It's kind of you to reassure me, Aunt Janet, but I know I'm at fault. It is as Rod says—I do not keep my attention firmly upon the main issue: the riding school. I had no business running off to Astley's like a foolish child, and then forgetting the time."

"But you were waiting to see the owner, were you not?" Janet asked, unconsciously revealing that she had overheard most of the altercation between the young people.

Chloe nodded. "Yes, Mrs. Astley gave me permission to wait to show Amigo to her husband. Oh, Aunt Janet," she said, her voice breaking a little. "Amigo is such a darling, and he has overcome his fear and hatred so beautifully! I have the feeling he should be given his chance at—at glory." Embarrassed, she smiled at the older woman. "If you could have seen him today, preening and prancing about under the admiring eyes of the entertainers! They appreciated his beauty and wit—and he *knew* it. I was so happy for him!"

Janet nodded decisively. "Then you must make a choice, my dear. Or perhaps I mean to say, put your goals in proper order. Which must come first, since I know the riding school has been a dream for you since you were a small child. Which of the two projects can wait?"

Put that way, the problem became simple for Chloe. She could always work to build the school, and perhaps if Amigo could be trained to perform, she might come by enough money to finance the riding academy eventually. And might not the limited fame she might achieve as an equestrienne be an assistance in advertising the school? Feeling appreciably better, she gave Janet the first spontaneously happy smile of the evening.

"Yes! I begin to see my way clear—thanks to your wisdom and kindness. You have been so good to me, dear Aunt Janet!"

"I meant to be better," quoth that good dame briskly. "Now tell me without roundaboutation, what have you decided to do?"

"Why, I think I shall remove to London, with Amigo and the mare, Molly, find me a hostel, and offer myself to work with Amigo at Astley's. If the Sergeant-Major will not accept me as a performer or a pupil, I can work in the stable and paddock. I've done so for years at my uncle Ned's farm.'

This announcement came as an unpleasant surprise. It was not part of Janet's plan to lose the girl so soon. Rallying, the older woman pursed her lips. "Not quite good enough, my dear. There are aspects of the situation you have not yet considered. I do not think your mother would have wished you to live alone in London, even in a good hostel—if you can find one in the city," she sniffed. "No, I believe I must accompany you. We shall find a small place, just a few rooms, together, and I shall cook and do what other housekeeping is necessary."

"Oh, no!" protested the girl. "I could not take you away from your lovely home at Kindlewick—and from your care of Rod! He would never be able to go on without you!"

"You think not?" asked Janet, pleased by the comment. "He has not himself expressed that view. Like all men, he takes much for granted. It might not do him any harm to see how he goes on without me for awhile."

Chloe's distress was obvious. "He would never forgive me!" she blurted, her face pale with alarm.

"I wonder?" mused Janet, growing more and more enamored of the idea. "I think we will try it and see." It might bring Rod to his senses, and precipitate matters between these two stubborn young people.

"But Aunt Janet—!" Chloe began.

"My mind is made up. We pack tomorrow, and leave the day after. That will give me time to find my replacement, and to send Alan to reserve a room at McLeod's Hotel in London while we look about us for a suitable lodging. Now, off to bed with you, child; you have had a tiring day! Excursions and alarums!"

"But the students!" Chloe cried. "I was forgetting them again!"

"We'll notify them that there will be a temporary suspension of the lessons," said Janet soothingly. "Good night!"

Lying in her comfortable bed in the dark, Chloe realized miserably that although it was good common sense to act as she and Janet had decided, her heart craved a different answer. If only Rod had liked her! If only she could stay, and be with him, seeing his cool blue eyes, his golden curls, and the big strong body that moved with such manly strength and grace! But of course it was impossible, for everything she did seemed to put him in a temper. He had never really liked or trusted her since Reggie spewed out his cowardly lies. All spoiled! cried her lonely heart. She wept a little, the unaccustomed tears burning. She had not known the experience of being valuable and important to anyone since her mother died. And even with her mother, she had been the one to protect and comfort the older woman, rather than the reverse. Chloe sighed, then got up and washed her face. She got back into bed, willing herself to sleep so she would be rested to cope with

138

tomorrow's problems. There would be her own packing, and Janet's . . .

She was still awake when, just before dawn, she heard Rod go quietly down the stairs to the kitchen. It did not enter her mind to wonder how she knew his step. She rose and dressed hastily. Whatever else she did or did not do, she knew that she could not leave Kindlewick Farm without making her peace with its owner, and trying to express her gratitude for the opportunity he had offered her to establish himself in her riding school.

Within a few minutes, Rod looked up from the table where he was dealing with a large bowl of the oatmeal porridge which Janet always had simmering on the stove. The single lamp above the table cast shadows over his face while it touched his bright hair to gold. He regarded the slender, pale little figure with a closed expression. Chloe had no idea what he was thinking. She came a few steps into the room. Still he did not speak.

"Rod—Mr. McLeod—" she faltered.

"Rod will do nicely," the man said.

"Thank you. Rod, I am going to leave for London tomorrow," she began.

"Are you going to meet someone there?" His question came out harshly.

"No! Not meet—that is—your Aunt Janet is going with me," Chloe blurted the information she had been dreading to impart.

For a wonder he did not seem as angry as she had expected. "I've no doubt the two of you will make a fine mull of it," he said, "and when you're ready to call for help, I *may* be willing to come and rescue you." Chloe was surprised to see the ghost of a smile tugging at the corners of his mouth.

"But I did not try to take her from you," Chloe urged, not quite understanding his attitude.

"Oh, she's been hankering to get off to the metropolis for months," Rod said. "You have given her an excuse. When she's tired of her little holiday, she'll come running back. This is her home as well as mine."

"But I was worried for you," confessed Chloe softly.

The idea seemed to interest him. "Were you, now?" he asked softly. "And what does that mean?"

"Your meals—the proper running of your home—" stammered the girl.

"And you think I'm dependent upon any woman for that?" Rod asked.

Chloe didn't like the tone of his voice. She met his eyes challengingly. "Yes, I think you will miss her care and her services very much."

"I will never miss anything a woman does not want to give me freely," Rod answered. Then with a queer little smile, he added, "I may even have another— lady—in mind to take care of my needs," he finished softly, in the voice Chloe didn't like at all. "Tell my aunt there will be no need for her to hurry back to me," he advised, still smiling into her face.

Chloe did not understand the emotions which buffeted her. "Well, whoever she is, I hope she burns your bacon and begrudges your tea!" she snapped, and ran from the room. Behind her, she heard Rod's laughter. "I shall *never* come back!" she vowed.

The packing went on apace that morning, with the two ladies bustling about giving every evidence of delighted anticipation of the visit to London. Unfortunately, the gentleman whom they were seeking to impress had made himself scarce, to their considerable annoyance. The afternoon, however, was marked by a most significant and gratifying event.

The housemaid came into the parlor where the ladies

140

were recruiting their strength with tea and scones to announce that there were two gentlemen to see Mr. Roderick McLeod, and did Miss McLeod know where he was to be found? Janet rose to the emergency, desiring the girl to bring the gentlemen in and then send one of the stableboys to look for his master. She urged Chloe to remain to lend moral support with the strangers, "For I will hazard a guess," she explained, "that these may be parents of two more pupils, and you, my love, will know better how to deal with them than I."

The gentlemen, when they presented themselves, were big, well-standing men in somber black clothing, both with a solemn, even stern, expression. They did not seem best pleased at being faced with two women rather than the man they had come to see.

Janet rose to welcome them. "Och, 'tis you, Cameron McLeod," she greeted one of them. "And this gentleman, if I mistake not, is my cousin Willie! Be seated, if you please, gentlemen. The tea is ready."

While the gentlemen rather stiffly acceded to her request—Chloe was of the opinion that they would have preferred something stronger and more in the national character than tea—Janet introduced the girl, and explained to her, "Mr. Cameron McLeod was my brother Angus's factor, and now serves the same capacity for my nephew."

Janet murmured all that was suitable, and passed the filled teacups and scones to the guests. Although they accepted the food and drink, the gentlemen did not relax their mutual air of dour formality, and were able to parry all Janet's skillful probing to discover the nature of their business with Rod. Finally she asked them.

The appalled looks the men gave each other at this display of feminine curiosity tickled Chloe's sense of humor. Eyes alight with laughter, she watched them hemming and hawing. Mr. Cameron McLeod was finally understood to say that as his errand was both private and official, it would be impossible for him to tell her anything about it. Since he added that Mr. Roderick McLeod would doubtless tell her whatever was needful for her to know, it was probably as well that Rod himself came in at that moment. The ladies excused themselves, Janet with icy civility and Chloe with suppressed amusement. No noticeable regret was observable in the expressions of the visitors at their departure.

Janet seized Chloe's wrist and pulled her into the kitchen, where she turned a face of outrage upon the girl. Chloe could no longer contain her laughter.

"Oh, Aunt Janet! When you came right out and demanded to know their business, I thought your cousin Willie would faint!" Overcome by the memory, she went off into another peal of laughter. After glaring at her for a moment, Janet began to chuckle.

"I had forgotten how angry a Scotsman could make me!" she confessed.

"Roderick being such a pattern-card of compliance and easy acquiescence!" teased Chloe.

"It's as well I've a sense of humor," Janet said, shaking her head. "Of all the pompous windbags—! I wonder what their mysterious business is?"

"Perhaps your other nephew is making an attempt to get Rod to return to Scotland?" suggested the girl.

"It could be, I suppose," admitted Janet. "Or perhaps he seeks a loan! Clutch-fisted penny-pincher!"

But the girl was frowning. "Rod wouldn't go back, would he? How could he abandon this magnificent farm and return to Scotland to be a younger brother without authority?"

Janet was in agreement that such a role would be impossible to conceive of in relation to Roderick McLeod.

She added, comfortably, "Ah, well, when all the *private and official* business is completed, we shall hear what the great matter was. One thing you may be sure of, it will make no difference to Rod's running of Kindlewick Farm!"

Janet McLeod could not have been more mistaken.

During the excellent dinner that evening, which the visitors were pleased to approve, nothing was said of the purpose of their foray into the alien country of the Sassenachs. Under Janet's sprightly lead, the talk was mostly of old friends and relatives—not, as Janet told Chloe later, in the class of a comfortable coze, but better than no news at all! Rod, big and courtly at the head of his table, was more restrained in manner than Chloe had ever seen him. The ladies very properly withdrew when the port was brought to the table. Chloe was ready to go to her room at once, since she intended leaving for London very early in the morning. Aunt Janet caught her arm as she turned toward the stairs.

"I think we'd better wait in my room upstairs," she said softly. "During dinner tonight, Rod gave me the signal he'd something to tell us."

"To tell *you*, surely," protested Chloe. "It must be to do with the news your visitors brought—family matters—"

"Can you assure me you've no curiosity at all about these mysteries?" teased Janet. "I, for one, am agog to hear the great news!"

In the event, the ladies had a long wait, for the visiting gentlemen were impressed with the quality of Mr. McLeod's liquor, and did it justice. It was past eleven when the impatient women heard the uneven footsteps mounting the stairs, and Rod's deep voice

143

advising and shepherding his guests to their rooms. A few minutes later there was a soft tapping on Janet's door. She flung it open.

"At last!" she breathed crossly. "Did they have to empty every bottle in the cellar?"

Rod grinned. The only sign of his own potations was a slight glitter in the blue eyes and a rather guilty smile on the well-cut mouth.

"Now, Janet love," he said softly, coming into the room and closing the door gently behind him, "is that any way to speak to the Laird?"

Janet's hands flew to her lips.

Rod squared his great shoulders. "I had thought you might have guessed. Brother Angus had a bad fall from his horse a month since, and has finally been gathered to his fathers. It seems, willy-nilly, I am the new head of the clan—for what that is worth."

Janet dropped her nephew a deep curtsy. He held out his right hand and lifted her up.

"My loyalty to you," she said in a gruff voice.

Rod smiled at her warmly. "If there's one thing in this business I *am* sure of, it's your loyalty," and kissed her cheek gently.

They seemed to have forgotten the girl.

"Will you have to return to Scotland?" asked Janet, frowning.

Rod considered the question soberly. "Cameron wishes me to, of course. They none of them ever accepted the fact that my life, my home, my interests are here, not with a few acres of stony hillsides and fog-draped mountains. I'd far rather bring the few clansmen we have left down here, and set them up in comfortable little crofts of their own." He rubbed his hand around the back of his neck, stretching to relieve the tired muscles. "I suppose I shall have to go up there for long enough to straighten things out. Cam tells me that the land is in bad heart—everything at sixes and sevens. . . . Angus was just like our father, I'm afraid—a very poor manager."

"I know one is not supposed to speak ill of the dead—although I am not clear why, for they can't hear one and be hurt by it!—but since neither Angus nor I have ever had a good word for one another, I surely will not make a pious pretense of grief now! Your brother Angus was the most unpleasant human being I have ever had the misfortune to meet—and it is just like him to have died in time to ruin my first holiday in London!" snapped Janet angrily.

Rod's eyebrows lifted. "But what nonsense is this? If you think you are going to return to the Towers with me . . . get a chill in that drafty barn of a place—! You'll go off for your holiday in London as you planned, and be ready to return and serve your Laird with renewed vigor and deference!" He chuckled. "Do you think I haven't a very good idea what I should have to put up with if I prevented you from taking this trip to London? I should never hear the end of it, and be served martyrdom with every meal!"

Janet laughed too, but reluctantly. "Well, I'll go for a wee while; and get Chloe suitably established near the Astleys, but then I'll come home and help you if you plan to relocate the rest of the family." She shook her head. "So many of Torquil McLeod's blood scattered across the face of the earth! Our branch of the clan is nearly extinct!"

"Then we must needs found a new house in this new land!" smiled Rod.

"In the heart of enemy territory?" jibed his aunt. "Among the Sassenachs?"

"The better the place, the better the deed," Rod paraphrased. He smiled warmly and held out both hands. "Will you help me?"

145

Watching him, Chloe felt her heart swelling with a new and painful emotion. Though she had never been to Scotland, and knew nothing of the clans, she understood how Janet had felt when she made obeisance to this splendid youth and pledged him her loyalty. *"Oh, if he would only ask me to help him!"* she thought, despairingly. *"How quickly I would agree!"* But he would not, of course. And what help could a poor little dab of a woman have to offer to such as Roderick McLeod?

Chapter Twelve

CHLOE SLIPPED OUT to the stables before dawn to inform Amigo of the coming move. The huge dark liquid eyes regarded her with interest, and the stallion seemed to say that he would be pleased to go venturing to the city with her, especially since he was to have a chance to shine in the arena. In fact his whole demeanor was so clearly complacent that Chloe began to suspect Amigo had been informed of the treats in store by someone else. Her suspicions were confirmed as a huge figure moved out of the shadows cast by the stable lantern and approached the stall.

"Having a chat with Amigo?" drawled Rod.

"What are you doing up at this hour?" snapped Chloe, ungraciously.

"I am frequently up at this hour," retorted her host imperturbably, "supervising the wagons as they leave for London. I have a business to run, you know."

The girl was at once apologetic. "I do know—and I

am truly grateful for the time and trouble you have spent upon my wretched affairs. It must have been a great bother to you!"

"I have managed to endure it," Rod said dryly.

Chloe wished rather forlornly that the big man would say he would miss her, even a little, but his closed, courteous expression revealed nothing of the feelings he might be experiencing. "He is most likely eager to be rid of me and my obstinate starts," she thought gloomily. Really, this early hour was most depressing! It made everything look darker and less happy! She lifted her gaze to meet the inquiring blue stare of her host. One golden eyebrow was lifted quizzically.

"Having second thoughts, young Chloe?" he murmured.

"No!—That is, I do not understand at all what you are asking," stammered the girl unhappily.

Rod subjected her to a searching scrutiny. "Ye're a stubborn wee lassie, ye ken verra weel," he said finally, in the outrageously broad Scots burr which always so much delighted her. A smile broke the sadness of her expression, and the big man nodded briskly. "Who canna learn by science must learn by suffering," he tossed off the aphorism. "Now back to the hoose for a wee bite of breakfast, lass. Ye'll need strength to enable ye to tackle the hazards of the great city. I'll see to Molly and Amigo. Off ye go, then!"

"Oh, Rod!" breathed the girl, not at all sure she could bear to part from this infuriating, endearing man.

But Rod had his own plans, and was in no mood to allow his timetable to be upset by any shilly-shallying female. "Off with ye, lassie! Your great adventure awaits, and, I have no doubt, so does Aunt Janet! I'd no want to be responsible for keeping her cooling her heels in the coach while ye dawdle about in the stables!"

Thus rebuked, Chloe fled to the house, feeling, most irrationally, as though her last friend had deserted her. Very cross at herself for indulging in such missish emotions, she was even crosser with Rod for being so calm and cheerful at the thought of her departure.

In spite of her dark thoughts, the leave-taking was amicable enough. Rod had arranged for Matt to drive them in a coach. It was an old-fashioned vehicle, musty and not too well sprung, but it held all their luggage in its capacious boot. Alan was to come with them, to ride Molly and lead Amigo through the light traffic of early morning to the Hotel McLeod.

Aunt Janet was her usual brisk, competent self, her stylish gray traveling cloak set off by a bright red flower. Rod, who was, in Chloe's opinion, looking unforgivably cheerful, bent to place a kiss on his aunt's cheek before he helped her into the carriage. "Have a pleasant holiday," he advised her, smiling. Then he turned to Chloe.

"Good-bye, Miss Keith," he said formally, offering her his hand to assist her to mount the high step into the coach. Then, abruptly, he caught her slight body close against his massive frame and pressed his mouth over her lips hard enough to bruise them.

"That is so you won't forget who's the Laird," he said outrageously, his smile mocking. Then he boosted Chloe bodily into the coach, and shut the door decisively after her. He was walking away before Matt had time to start the team.

The coach rumbled down the lane and lurched onto the highway as Chloe, fuming, straightened her bonnet and pelisse and settled herself into her seat. She cast a darkly glowering eye at Aunt Janet. That good dame nodded sympathy.

"It is ever thus with the male sex, I have found," she said judiciously. "They *must* have the last word, even if it involves throwing one into a vehicle and slamming a door to make sure of it." Chloe was thankful that the older woman had not commented upon the shocking action and speech which had immediately preceded the manhandling. She set herself to present a calm and cheerful appearance, and chatted brightly about the passing scene as the coach rumbled on toward the metropolis. However, when she heard herself commenting for the third time on the smoke which hung like a pall over the roofs of London, she faced her companion with tear-bright eyes. "I am so happy!" she announced. "I have dreamed of this moment since the day we visited Astley's. Amigo must be given his chance to shine!"

"I too have looked forward to this day," Janet confided. "I need a little town bronze. I have become sadly rustic—a veritable gapeseed. A few months of the pleasures of London—museums, concerts, the libraries —and I shall feel alive again."

Having thus sought to convince each other of their complete satisfaction at leaving Kindlewick and its master, both ladies lapsed into a depression, and Chloe, staring blindly out of the window at the sights of the metropolis, found herself seeing instead a pair of challenging blue eyes and a strong, tanned face beneath a thatch of yellow curls.

It took Aunt Janet a surprisingly short time to get the two ladies comfortably settled into new quarters in an old, rambling house near the Royal Grove. It was a boarding house, offering two clean, neat rooms and three tasty meals a day in return for a sum of money which alarmed Chloe, unused as she was to city prices. However, Janet assured her it was very reasonable indeed, compared to the McLeod Hotel, at which they had stayed for less than a week.

"The chief virtue of this place," she commented,

looking about her at the rather dingy dining room in which they sat, "is its close proximity to Astley's. I am grateful to Rod for arranging rooms for us at the McLeod Hotel, but it would not do for you to have to jaunter across London every day on your way to practice with Amigo. That would be foolish beyond permission! Your strength must be saved for your work." She cast a speculative glance at the girl. "Besides, while we stayed at the hotel, my overbearing nephew had access to more information about us than was good for him."

"You—you think he might have set up an intelligencer—?"

"No, not that. But I'm sure that every single body on the staff, from McLeod down, would be eager to report to Rod all our doings, to say nothing of our comings and goings. They'd think it their duty to the Laird."

There was a little silence as the last word reverberated in the dining room, recalling to both ladies the final comment of Rod's just before the coach left. To Janet's regret, however, Chloe did not rise to the bait, but merely wiped her lips with the linen napkins Janet provided for their use at each meal, and then said, in a subdued voice, that it was time for her to return to the Royal Grove.

Janet was not best pleased by her young companion's appearance these days. For whatever reason, the small face seemed pinched and tired, and Chloe's usual cheerful manner was oddly muted. Still, the girl was obviously enjoying her work with Amigo, who was now comfortably established in Astley's stables, where he was by way of thinking himself to be the leader of the herd, having already offered a shrill challenge to all of the Sergeant-Major's stallions. Nothing serious had come of Amigo's arrogance, since Astley knew horses too well to permit close confrontations with his precious, high-mettled performers. Still, there was no denying that Amigo was a rare and remarkable talent.

Chloe discovered that she had been correct in her feeling that Amigo was a natural clown. He was tirelessly inventive—a true comic—and if some of his tricks left her shaken and occasionally bruised, there was no malice in him. Astley, watching the fun, shook a regretful head. "If only I had been able to train him from a foal! He's up to any lark, and more intelligent than the average, I promise you! Still, perhaps his buffoonery will be more entertaining than the formal routines I might have taught him. You say he'd been ill-treated before you got him?"

Chloe related once more the story of the sadistic squire. Astley, frowning, ran his big hand gently over the stallion's scars. "Battle decorations," he murmured. "Remarkable he didn't become a killer." He eyed the girl narrowly. She was holding Amigo's headstall, and the animal, with an exaggerated sigh, dropped his great head onto her shoulder with a thump which staggered the girl. Chloe met Astley's grin with a rueful smile.

"He's such a showoff!" she explained. "He doesn't mean to hurt me."

Astley agreed. "He's devoted to you—as he should be. It's thanks to you he's still alive, not put down as a killer. Now what is this act you and he have been practicing? Mrs. A. tells me it's a winner."

Chloe mounted Amigo and gave him their secret signal. The great stallion was delighted to cooperate. He enjoyed their games very much indeed, and obviously thought himself quite a performer. First he pranced delicately around the ring, shivering in exaggerated and quite spurious fright at several shadows, and at the grinning attention of the acrobats, riders, and stableboys who stopped as usual to watch his antics. One of the grooms obliged him by waving an arm and hopping up and down. Amigo, recognizing the signal, rolled his eyes to show the whites, reared on his powerful hind legs and put on a very convincing performance of a terrified horse. He shied, whinnied, caracoled, frog-leaped. Then he took off at a gallop around the ring, the picture of a panic-stricken steed. Through all this pantomime, Chloe sat quietly on his broad back, a small imperturbable image.

Then, with a touch of one heel, she directed him to the hurdle over which they had been practicing. Astley, frowning, noted its height. On the other side of it, simulating a water jump, was a wide, deep pile of straw mattresses. Astley stepped forward with a hand raised in objection, but the girl had already started her final run. Gathering the great beast together with the lightest touch of rein and heel, she set him at the hurdle. Powerful muscles bunched, then stretched as Amigo took the high jump with triumphant mastery.

Then it happened. At the crucial moment, some indecision seemed to attack the tiny rider. Throwing up her hands as in terror, she tumbled from the horse's back and landed with an audible thump on the pile of mattresses. There was a theatrical silence in the great arena. Astley hurried toward the spot, half in fear and half in reluctant admiration. The girl must have been getting instruction from the tumbler's and acrobats—if indeed the fall was intentional!

But Chloe and Amigo had not concluded the act. The great horse, stretching his powerful neck and prancing forward self-consciously, bent to the small, still figure on the mattresses. Grasping the heavy collar of her shirt in careful teeth, he lifted her from the mattresses and dragged her to a point in good view of the stands. Then he deposited her on the tanbark. Lifting his head, he gave such an extravagant whinnying chuckle of mirth that the spectators were convulsed with sympa-

153

thetic laughter. Much encouraged, Amigo tossed his head and repeated the whinny.

"The original horse-laugh," noted Astley, helping a triumphant if winded Chloe to her feet. "I salute a master trainer," he continued. "I'll add the act to the program. I wouldn't want that rascal Hughes stealing you away from me."

Charles Hughes, another riding-master, had started a rival exhibition, and was papering the town with posters which made mock of Sergeant-Major Astley's much publicized, grandiloquent claims. So there was more anger than amusement in Astley's comment, however he had meant it. The ubiquitous Hughes was getting under his skin. Chloe hastened to reassure him.

"I am more than grateful to you and to Mrs. Astley for your kindness, your interest in my amateur performance, and the skills you have permitted me to learn from your fine artists," she said earnestly. The Sergeant-Major inspected her small, serious face.

"You are a very quick pupil, Miss Keith," he complimented her. "I am surprised and gratified at what you have accomplished in so short a time." He glanced at the complacent Amigo, now the center of an admiring coterie. "That's a horse in a million," he added. "He'll earn you enough to establish your little riding school on the outskirts of London, which is what I'm aware you have in mind."

"You aren't—angry?" ventured the girl.

"Why should I be?" protested Astley. "Mrs. Astley told me right at the start what your plan was. I'm sure it's best for you, considering that both you and Amigo are a little too old to be trained in my skills."

"Oh." At first Chloe felt just a little pique at his rather cavalier estimation of her potential, but common sense, of which she had an ample supply, soon counseled her that he was exactly right. And for all the fun Amigo was having, she could hardly sacrifice her own life's ambition for longer than a few months. Just long enough to make the money to establish her school, she promised herself. That would show certain arrogant persons that a woman could manage her own affairs without help from some overbearing male." 'Forget who's the Laird,' indeed!" Well, Chloe Keith was no clanswoman of his, that was sure—to be owing him any sort of allegiance! Arrogant creature! She went off into a brown study, imagining herself telling the impossible man what she really thought of his pretensions. Astley, noting her abstraction, shrugged goodnaturedly and strolled away to his office to argue with his wife over the cost of having some new posters printed which should utterly demolish the ridiculous claims of the miserable Hughes, and convince the public of the superiority of Astley's production.

Chloe collected the lionizing Amigo and gave him into the charge of an admiring groom to be taken to the stables, cooled off, brushed down and fed. "Give him an extra bait of corn," she suggested. "He did me proud today."

"That he did, the rascal," agreed the groom. "He's got as good an opinion of himself as our Sergeant-Major has!"

Chloe made her way back to the boarding house with determined steps. It would be only fair to share with Aunt Janet the story of this morning's success. The older woman had been a perfect companion: occupying herself with her own interests, sharing these when she felt they would be attractive to her young companion, but never making herself any kind of a burden or obligation to Chloe. The girl felt love and gratitude for this dear friend of her mother's. Was it perhaps selfish to keep Janet from her comfortable home at Kindlewick?

Chloe set her lips. Today was as good a time as any to lay all the cards on the table.

When Chloe arrived, Aunt Janet had just finished dressing to go out to Montagu House to see the art collection and library of Sir Hans Sloane, recently acquired by the government. She had ordered a carriage to drive her to the city, but had no hesitation in dismissing it when she saw the look on Chloe's face. To the girl's half-hearted protestations, she returned a crisp answer.

"It's plain to see you've a bee or two in your bonnet, my dear. Whatever's happened, you shall tell me all about it, and we'll decide together what's to be done. Now, suppose you try to persuade our redoubtable landlady to provide us with a cup of tea, and possibly a few sandwiches, and we'll discuss the matter in comfort."

Chloe regarded the older woman with affection as she ate one of the hearty sandwiches she had ordered. "I *was* hungry, Aunt Janet! These are most sustaining," and she finished one and selected another.

Janet's eyes smiled over the rim of her teacup. "Everything tends to look brighter upon a full stomach," she murmured. "Now, open your budget, child! What has happened at the Royal Grove?"

Chloe chewed, swallowed, then nodded her head. "It is really good news, Aunt, but it presents me with a problem—or perhaps I should say, with a decision to be made."

"Tell all," encouraged Aunt Janet. She had continually to congratulate herself upon her wisdom in bringing Chloe to London. The child seemed to attain new maturity daily, although she was still somewhat pale and prone to long silences. However, since Janet thought she knew exactly the reason for this behavior, she was not too worried about the state of her charge. And as for herself, she would not have missed the intellectual and artistic stimulation she had received in London. Still, enough was enough, and perhaps it was time to consider getting the girl back to Kindlewick—and Roderick McLeod. So she repeated briskly, "Tell me all."

"Well, first, Amigo had his chance to perform before Mr. Astley today. It was," she said complacently, "a triumph!"

Janet chuckled in sympathy. "I can just see him, every elegant inch the star."

"Indeed, he knew his worth!" agreed Chloe, smiling. "Mr. A. was much impressed, and offered us a chance to be in the show. At a salary—so that I could save up to open my own school. Mrs. A. had discussed it with him, and he felt it was my best course." She hesitated, then finished in a more somber tone. "Since, he said, both Amigo and myself are too old to be properly trained as a trick riding team."

Aunt Janet concealed her deep relief at this fortunate decision, and said all that was proper in praise of the horse and his mistress. "So you are to perform your comedy ride at the Royal Grove? I shall be in a front seat for your opening night, I promise you!" She leaned over and gave the sober-looking Chloe a gentle kiss upon the cheek. "How long do you plan to perform?"

"I should think a couple of months would be long enough to bring my savings to the required amount," answered Chloe. "Thanks to you and—and Rod," she stumbled a little over the name, "I have not been allowed to touch my inheritance from Uncle Ned Brown. The sum should be enough for what I have in mind."

"You are not thinking of leaving Kindlewick, I hope?" said Janet firmly. "Neither Rod nor I would permit it! I, because of my promises to your mother."

"You think Rod would be willing to let me stay?" murmured the girl, not looking at Janet.

"My dear child, he is exactly like his father and all the men of the clan McLeod in *that*," said Janet. "He cannot bear to see one of his own escaping from his control—"

"But I am not . . . am not . . . *his own*," murmured the girl, then looked up through her lashes at Janet hopefully.

The older lady appeared to be considering this seriously. After a moment she said, "I wonder if you can have forgot a rather significant remark my nephew made just as we were leaving Kindlewick! Something to the effect that he wished you to be sure to remember that he was your Laird?" She paused to scrutinize the rosy, worried little face across the table from her.

Chloe frowned. "But he *isn't*," she said slowly. "I have nothing to do with Clan McLeod. By birth," she added.

"No, not by birth," Aunt Janet agreed almost too cheerfully.

"Then—?"

"There are other ways of being incorporated into a clan than by birth," Janet said firmly.

Chloe waited. The older woman did not elaborate upon her very provocative thesis. Finally, Chloe asked desperately, "Aunt Janet! What—other ways?"

"Well, there's adoption," began Janet solemnly, then gave up and chuckled. "Child, the boy dotes on you," she said. "*Surely* you noticed?"

"Dotes?" sputtered Chloe. "When he loses no opportunity to insult and hector, snub and browbeat me?"

"Just as I said," corroborated Janet, chuckling. "The great silly gowk thinks that's the way to gain your attention."

"He's done that, I'll admit." Chloe pondered the matter while Janet watched her with amusement. "Well, if you are right—and you *do* have the advantage of

158

having lived in the same house and observed his behavior!—then I must surely be very high on his list, for he's lost no opportunity to bullock me!" A sudden thought struck her, not too pleasantly if the scowl on her face was any indication. "I suppose he has quite a stable of young females he browbeats upon every occasion?"

Janet laughed. "No, oddly enough, Rod hasn't seemed to be much in the petticoat line. In fact, my dear Chloe, you are the first girl I've ever heard him be so rude to."

"I suppose I should be flattered that he bothered to vent his spleen so freely upon me," muttered the girl. "What a splendid prospect for any woman so foolish as to have him for a husband! A lifetime of vilification!"

"Well, now, my dear, I would not go so far as that," answered Janet. "In fact, from my observation of the man, I would venture to say that he'll spoil his wife thoroughly. Of course, he would be sure to demand her whole dependence and attention."

Chloe privately considered that it would not at all be difficult to devote one's whole attention to the reprehensible Roderick, but forebore to say this to his aunt, who might, through a mistaken sense of loyalty to her nephew, be moved to repeat it. Instead she tossed her head and said she was sure she pitied any poor wretch who found herself shackled to that great bully.

"Just so, my dear," agreed Janet, much heartened by this conversation.

Chapter Thirteen

THE RETURN FROM SCOTLAND to the broad smiling fields and prosperous affairs of Kindlewick filled Rod with a real sense of homecoming. But he soon found that something was wrong. The farm had never seemed so empty, which was odd in view of the fact that the whole staff and working force was present as usual, with the exception of the housekeeper. "Surely," Rod asked himself in considerable annoyance, "the absence of Aunt Janet cannot create this feeling of emptiness—of loss?"

As the days passed, and the only intelligence he received from the city was an occasional wretched scrawl from his aunt, which said nothing about anything of importance, but merely bibble-babbled on about museums and art galleries, Rod's temper, never equable, became extremely exacerbated. He was seriously considering the notion of riding into London to see for

himself what ploys the silly females were about, when
he had a very disturbing visitor.

Lord Randal Beresford rode in one Saturday morning, looking, Rod considered, a great deal too well
pleased with himself and a good deal more handsome
than any man had a right to be. After a brief and not
too friendly exchange of greetings, Lord Randal handed
Rod a large, rolled-up poster.

"I wondered how much you knew about this, McLeod,"
was the rather censorious comment with which the
poster was offered.

Rod unrolled the garish thing. It advertised Sergeant-
Major Astley's Greatest Performance, including Acts of
Horsemanship, with interludes of "tumbling, rope-
dancing and Chinese shadows, and the Egyptian pyr-
amids, an amusing performance of men piled upon men
to form a living triangle." Rod was about to inquire
rudely what all this nonsense had to do with him, when
his eyes caught a familiar name near the bottom of the
poster. "Special Added Attraction!!" screamed the lurid
print. "Little Miss Chloe Keith, Child Equestrienne,
mounted upon Amigo, Prince of Equine Clowns, in
their sparkling Comic Interlude!"

" 'Child Equestrienne'!" gritted the affronted McLeod.
"I'll give her a comic interlude when I lay hands upon
her!"

"Just so," said Lord Randal. "Infuriating, isn't she?
But I admit I wondered whether you might have encouraged her in this—"

Rod's look of outrage reassured him.

"Is it that she needs the money?" persisted his lordship.

Mr. McLeod was understood to say that he had more
than enough for anything the girl might need, including her riding school.

"Then I think, if you are truly intending to wed her,
it is time you curbed her propensity for making a

161

public show of herself," stated his lordship crisply.

Rod wore a brow of thunder. "Ye may rest easy on that score, Beresford," he snarled, with a truly formidable rolling of his r's. "I'll be away off to London at once, and when I get my hands upon those two silly females, I'll—" Words failed him.

"Nothing irreversible, I trust," murmured Lord Randal.

"I'll *sorrrrrrt* them both," promised the Highlander, and the way he said it, it did indeed seem a formidable threat.

"If you fail to do so," offered Milord, "perhaps I should try my-er-powers of persuasion."

"And just what does yer lorrrrdship mean by that rrremarrrrk?" challenged Rod, his Scots burr becoming thicker as his temper rose.

"It means," retorted Lord Randal, succinctly, "that I'll handle her if you can't."

"May I live to see the day!" sneered Rod. "The way the story reached me, she did exactly as she pleased from the moment you met her, and you were unable to stop her, the wild wee limmer! I also heard you were mightily pleased to be rid of her at Kindlewick Farm! Your leave-taking, I am reliably informed by Miss McLeod, was more notable for haste than courtesy." He brushed aside Milord's bristle of repudiation. "As to your 'handling her,'" Rod continued, "I'm wondering what the Lady Barbara would have to say to that? Or had you intended to keep your activities a secret?"

Both men were glaring like angry bulls by now. There was a determined light of battle in Milord's eyes, and an unholy joy upon Rod's face as they advanced upon one another.

"Yoo-hoo! Mr. McLeod!" a shrill female voice halted them in their tracks. Both young men turned to annihilate the feckless female who had dared to interrupt

at a time like this. They beheld a plump, modishly-attired woman approaching them, dragging a pair of reluctant little girls in her wake.

"I am Mrs. Eudosia Gibbon," she informed them, coyly. "Sir Peter Daley—*such* a dear man!—persuaded me to bring my nieces to your Riding Academy! He spoke of you so *highly*, Mr. McLeod! So I have brought Sophia and Honoria to you. They are so eager to learn to *ride!*" And she beamed impartially upon both of the handsome giants before her.

"It seems," breathed Milord, "we shall have to postpone our—discussion until a more convenient time. After all, you cannot keep Sophia and Honoria waiting, can you, Mr. McLeod?"

With visible reluctance Rod went forward to greet his unwelcome clients. He flicked a stormy, dark-blue glare at the grinning Lord Randal, ground out a choked, "Later, Milord! Ye've not heard the last o' this!" and then proceeded to ignore his lordship completely while he talked quietly with his two unwilling pupils.

Beresford lingered just long enough to see the swift conquest of the children, and to behold his almost-antagonist going off toward the stables, a little girl clinging trustfully to each large hand. Then, suddenly realizing his own danger, he directed the too-cordial Mrs. Gibbon to the parlor of the farmhouse and beat a hasty retreat.

As it happened, Rod did not attend the opening performance of Chloe and Amigo. By the time he had gotten rid of Mrs. Gibbon and her nieces, it was already well on into the afternoon, and sober second thoughts were counseling caution. He had a pretty clear idea of Chloe's reaction if he arrived, breathing fire, to haul her back to Kindlewick. A reluctant smile tugged at his lips. "She'd try to murder me, the wee tigress!" he thought. That might have its charm, but on the whole Rod preferred to come to terms with his chosen lady-love in a more romantic setting and under different circumstances than would exist during a wild brawl in front of half of London at Astley's circus. So Rod stayed at home, and missed a very surprising event.

Chloe's debut upon the Prince of Equine Clowns was all that the Sergeant-Major could have hoped. The large, enthusiastic audience was a heady stimulus to Amigo. His fine dark eye rolled in a histrionic frenzy, and he pranced and reared with all the dramatic fury of a Cheltenham tragedian. Chloe, sensing his elation, began to fear that he might get so far above himself as to become careless, and sought, by gentle touch and word, to restrain his enthusiasm. An actual water jump had been provided to take the place of the pile of mattresses for the final trick. Nothing was too difficult, or too extravagant, for Astley when he had an idea in his head, and the stableboys had spent the whole morning carrying buckets of water to fill the huge wood-lined trench the Sergeant-Major had had built in the center of the arena. To this water jump Amigo and Chloe now addressed themselves. The girl, clad in a gaudy mockery of a lady's riding habit, sat the great stallion with quiet poise. Amigo thundered down toward the hurdle, gathered himself together, leaped, and soared triumphantly over the hazard. Carrying out her part, Chloe shrieked, threw up her arms, and tumbled into the water. Then she pushed herself to the surface, turning so that the heavy corded collar of her costume would be easily available to Amigo's teeth.

True to his training, Amigo pranced up to the water jump, pulled back his head in blatant surprise, and whickered inquiringly. The shocked silence which had greeted Chloe's spill began to be filled with comments and chuckles of amusement. Then Amigo, bending his great head, got a good grip on the prepared collar and hauled Chloe out of the water, holding her clear of the ground and mincing in wide circles which showed off the small girl's dripping form to the audience. Chloe remained limp, as they had practiced, but she had much to do to keep from reprimanding the horse for the evident pleasure he was getting out of her ludicrous position. When at last after two more circles than they had practiced he deposited her upon the tanbark, and backing off, gave his piercing horse-laugh, Chloe was almost ready to drown her stagestruck mount.

However, the audience's response was all that Astley could have hoped for. Gales of laughter and applause resounded in the building, and Amigo took numerous bows with all the greed of a seasoned actor. When Chloe finally got him out of the arena, she led him to the stables with less charity than she had ever felt. Handing him over to the grinning groom, she snapped, very conscious of the dripping garment which was plastered tightly to her skin, "I am glad that mountebank doesn't get to immerse me again until Monday evening! What a heartless wretch he is!"

Amigo whinnied plaintively, but Chloe was in no mood to indulge his histrionics. She left the stable and, deciding to return at once to the boarding house by way of the back alley, hastened through the dusk, holding her dripping riding skirt off the ground.

It was with a real shock that she heard the voice accosting her from the shadows. "Very amusing, Tiger!"

She whirled to face the speaker. Surely Lord Randal would not address her in that hatefully mocking tone? She peered into the shadows. Coming toward her was a foppishly dressed male . . . a gaunt body—a thin, dark sneering face—Chloe gasped. Sir Jerold Peke! She

165

turned to run. In a second he was beside her, his hand heavy on her arm.

"Oh, no, my dear Miss Chloe Keith, 'Child Equestrienne'! I shall not permit you to escape me again! Not until we have finished the business we began in Beresford's bedroom at that inn on the London road," said Sir Jerold. "No," as she struggled to free herself from his grasp, "you'll not get away till I give you leave! I have important matters to discuss with you—and for your sake, and that of your—*patron*," sneered the hateful voice, "I advise you to behave yourself."

Chloe's teeth were chattering, as much from distaste of Peke's clutch on her arm as from cold. "You must see, Sir Jerold, that I am drenched to the skin and should change at once. If you will tell me your business with me, briefly, perhaps we may arrange a future meeting in better circumstances." A meeting which she would *not* attend, she thought nervously, for the creature showed no sign of releasing her.

His words confirmed her fear. "You must indeed take me for a nodcock," laughed Sir Jerold. "I'll escort you to your caravan, or whatever place you use to change your clothes, and while you are getting into dry clothing, I'll tell you what I want."

This was decidedly threatening, Chloe realized. The night air was already making itself uncomfortably cold on her wet body, and some groom or stableboy might come out at any moment and discover her with this unpleasant man. Perhaps it might be best to take him back to the boarding house, where Aunt Janet would serve as a very efficient chaperone, and might even be capable of routing the fellow! Without further ado, Chloe turned and led the way by the alley to the rear of the building. There was a side door which led, by way of a little passage, to what had been the servants' stairway when the house had been a private dwelling.

166

Chloe led the man hastily up to the rooms she shared with Aunt Janet. The smaller of these had been converted by the older woman into a cozy little parlor, while the larger contained two beds, their clothing in a monstrous old armoire, and a very practical washstand with a commode.

Chloe unlocked the door and led the way into the parlor where a single lamp glowed against her return.

"Please be seated, sir," she said shortly. "I shall advise my aunt of your presence, and you may explain your business to her while I change."

Sir Jerold muttered an oath, and strode angrily after her. "What is this about an aunt?" he sneered, but there was a look of uncertainty on his narrow countenance. "I am sure you will not wish another woman to learn what I know about you?" He glanced around the comfortable yet spartan room. "Unless, of course, she is an 'Abbess,' " he concluded with a smirk.

Since Chloe had not come in the way of hearing that particular piece of vulgar cant, she cast a puzzled look over her shoulder as she was about to enter her bedroom. "An Abbess? Why no, she is not in Holy Orders. I thought you had seen her with me that afternoon at the Royal Grove?" She opened the bedroom door. "Aunt Janet? We are honored with a visit from Sir Jerold Peke—of whom I have told you."

Turning her back on Sir Jerold's sickly smirk, she entered the room and closed the door behind her. For it had been immediately apparent to her that the bedroom was empty. *Where was Aunt Janet?* Oh, gods! she had probably gone to Amigo's first performance, and might very well have remained for the rest of the show! Which meant, Chloe thought desperately, stripping her wet, revealing costume from her shivering body, that she was now alone with the horrid man she had so stupidly led to her private apartments! Could anything be more unfortunate, more degrading? Unless she could get rid of him quickly, she was not only compromised, but in real danger of being injured by the man who had not scrupled to strike her with his fist in Lord Randal's sickroom!

She struggled to get herself into a very demure, highnecked gown of heavy wool. Her trembling fingers were making slow work of fastening the buttons when a mocking voice asked, "Do you need any help? Or is the mythical Aunt Janet doing it for you?"

Whirling, she saw that Peke had followed her into the bedroom and was leaning against the closed door. On his face was a smile whose quality sent a hideous chill through the girl's breast.

"I had not intended advancing quite so rapidly in our acquaintanceship, not having been really sure what you are, but this invitation to your room tells me all I need to know," he said, and began to take off his coat.

"I thought she was here!" cried Chloe, in distress, and a stupider man than Peke would have realized she meant it. However, after a considering glance at the small, anxious face, he continued to remove his coat, saying briskly, "Well, we can both of us see she isn't, and perhaps, if you are very accommodating, I shall not offer you the harsh alternatives I had originally intended."

Chloe backed to the small table which stood between the beds and took up the lamp which lighted the room. "If you advance one step further I shall throw this at you! I may set the place afire, but you, at least, will get a nasty burn!"

Sir Jerold glared at her, his narrow face revealing his indecision. "You are a hell-cat!" he said at last. "Well, it is quite your own fault if I misunderstood. No decent woman would lead a man to her bedroom—but you have a habit of sharing a man's bedroom, have you not?" He turned back to the parlor as he spoke, and began to struggle into his coat. When he was well away from the door, Chloe followed him hastily out into the neutral area of the other room. He was making himself comfortable in Aunt Janet's chair, and looking as though he planned to remain for some time.

Chloe hesitated near the outer door. "I wish you will leave at once, Sir Jerold. There is nothing we can have to say to one another, I promise you."

"Oh, but there is something very important indeed which I have to say to you, my dear," grinned her tormentor. "It concerns a mutual *friend* of ours," and he chuckled knowingly as he pronounced the word. "Lord Randal Beresford, I mean. You will recall, I am sure, the occasion on which we three met, in—of all places!— Milord's room at the inn."

"He was suffering a concussion, and I was, though he did not know it, engaged in getting him to safety and medical care."

"He was in full possession of his senses, and you were sharing his bedroom—and had done so for at least two days," countered Peke.

"Nothing occurred of which either Lord Randal or myself could be ashamed," said Chloe proudly.

"You cannot expect me to believe that, nor will the quizzes of London. I am really unhappy when I think what this rumor will do to Milord's relationship with his fiancée, the Lady Barbara Dickson." He observed the girl's sudden pallor with a smile. "Oh, yes, that will put the cat among the pigeons, no mistake! Everyone humiliated, a nasty little scandal for the *Ton* to bandy about! Lady Barbara will be compelled to break off her engagement; dear Randal will be given the cold shoulder by all his acquaintance; and even more unfortunate, the golden dowry of his proposed bride will not materialize to settle his very pressing debts. Yes, I think a hasty retreat to the Continent for a few years will be the only course open to our unhappy *friend*."

"Why are you telling me all this?" whispered the girl. "Are you offering me a chance to prevent your spreading your lies?"

Sir Jerold regarded her broodingly. "You have a nasty tongue in your head, girl," he said grimly. "I had intended to take you on as my tiger, flaunt you around town under Beresford's nose, but since I find you are a circus performer, I suppose that aspect of your situation would not worry you."

"Aspect?" Chloe was holding on to her composure grimly, her mind darting around the situation in a frantic search for a loophole.

"A woman who would display herself as you did today before such a crowd—as good as naked when the horse pulled you out of the water—would scarcely be worried at the threat of a loss of reputation. So I have to revise my own plans. Now I think it would satisfy me just as well to tell Barbara of her perfect knight's involvement with a circus woman, traveling about the country with her, while pretending to be so devoted to his betrothed! That will set the tongues wagging! But it will also break her heart. She idealizes the fellow, you see."

"You would do this to someone who has never harmed you?" whispered the girl.

The fury of his response startled her. "Lord Randal has thwarted and insulted me more than once! I promised myself I would get even with him, and by God, I'm going to do it! Ruin his happiness, break his engagement, make him a laughingstock—!"

"I am sure many members of the Beau Monde have affairs with women they do not intend to wed," protested Chloe.

"But they don't let 'em be flaunted and noised about

the *Ton,*" retorted Peke. "Wilferd and I'll see that everyone knows what dear Randal is up to. We'll swear we caught him with you—he's been out to that farm often enough!"

"You are thoroughly despicable," said Chloe, quietly.

He sneered, but the ugly color came up into his face. "It might be wiser not to antagonize me, miss, since I hold all the cards!"

"What do you wish me to do?" asked Chloe. There would be time later to consider how Peke's news about Randal's engagement affected her; now she must get the worst of the situation clear, so she could decide how to act.

Her apparent capitulation caused Sir Jerold to relax. He sat back in Aunt Janet's chair and began to smile as he looked insolently at her body. "The notorious Child Equestrienne is worthy of higher position than my tiger," he began. "I am coming to think that there would be quite a cachet having a circus performer as my peculiar." He grinned. "You may begin to pack your things. I'll send a coach for you later tonight, and have you brought to my home." He caught her gesture of rejection. "Oh, I'll permit you to continue with your work at the Royal Grove. You're nothing if you're not performing for Astley. That's what'll make you interesting in the eyes of my friends."

"And if I agree to go to your home, you will sign a paper not to tell your lies about Lord Randal and myself?"

"Lies, my dear?" Sir Jerold had quite recovered his good spirits. His bold cast had been successful. When he tired of the chit he could always spread the story against Beresford; in the meantime it would be amusing to play with the girl—she must have something to her to interest a man like Beresford. And wouldn't old Wilferd open his eyes when he learned that Jerry had

171

netted an actress? Sir Jerold decided not to share this information with his friend until it was an accomplished fact. Smiling, he rose to his feet.

"I'll ride home now, but I'll be back with a carriage to pick you up in about two hours. Be ready. Pack only what you wish—I can probably be coaxed into buying you a few fripperies if you treat me very well." The fatuous smile faded from his mouth, to be replaced by a look of cruel anticipation. "And if you do not please me, there's always this," and he drove his clenched fist into the palm of his other hand. "How long did it take for the swelling to go down last time?" he mocked.

And then he was gone, and Chloe bent over, holding her arms around her shaking body, and collapsed into Aunt Janet's chair. The older woman found her there twenty minutes later when she returned from the arena.

Chapter Fourteen

ALTHOUGH SHE WAS SHOCKED and frightened by her encounter with Peke, Chloe quickly decided that she could not tell Aunt Janet what had happened. Her involvement with Lord Randal and his enemies had nothing to do with the McLeods, and they must not be worried by the stupid situations she seemed to be forever getting herself into. On the other hand, she was sure she could not permit Sir Jerold to *blackmail* her into becoming his mistress. Blackmail. An interesting word! Her mind welcomed the digression. She remembered her mother telling her about the tax the freebooters on the border of Scotland exacted from the farmers. And the moral to the story had been that you do not ever secure real safety by such payments.

Yet it was essential that Lord Randal should not suffer because of befriending her. Very well, then, she told herself, you owe him protection. But how was this to be accomplished?

It was at this point in her cogitations that Aunt Janet arrived back at the boarding house from the Royal Grove, and offered praise for Amigo's act, warm loving friendship, and a good hot cup of tea. This strengthened Chloe's resolve not to draw the McLeods into what was, after all, her own problem. So, putting on a bright face, the girl said, "I'm going to run out and fetch something from the city for Mrs. A. I'll be back within a couple of hours. And Aunt Janet, that awful Peke creature saw me at the performance and followed me home. I got rid of him, but he threatened to return. Why not lock the door? I'll call out when I return, so you'll know it's me."

"It's I," corrected Janet absently, not for one moment taken in by the girl's story but not wishing to add to whatever burden the child was carrying. She saw Chloe off cheerfully, then, after some thought, sat down and wrote a brief but forceful note to Rod, smiling grimly as she sealed it and took it downstairs to the parlor. "It will set him up unbearably to think we fragile creatures cannot get along without his masculine strength," she thought, "but what of that? We do need him, and he is capable of handling whatever the child has got herself into."

She paid the landlord's son a suitable amount to saddle up and take her note to Kindlewick Farm, and promised him a bonus if he did it quickly. Then she recruited the landlord's wife, and together they went to her rooms and prepared a welcome for the rascal Peke which should cause him to think twice before annoying a young girl in the future.

Chloe's plan was a simple one. The person most likely to be hurt by Peke's villainy was not, after all, Lord Randal or even herself. It was the lovely and

174

gracious and friendly Lady Barbara. Therefore it was to the Dickson townhouse that Chloe directed her hired carriage, and within a short space of time the vehicle had drawn up in front of an imposing mansion. Requesting the driver to wait, Chloe made her determined way to the massive front door. She was thankful to note that only the normal number of lamps were burning, and no red carpet stretched across the muddy street. Lord Dickson was not entertaining tonight, fortunately. Now if his daughter was only at home!

Again fortune smiled. The Lady Barbara was at home, her imposing butler admitted, but he would have to discover whether his mistress was at home to Miss Chloe Keith.

"I hope you will find that she is," said Chloe with her wide lovely smile. "You see, it is very important that I see her tonight."

The butler, being no more proof against that smile than any other man, made his stately way to the drawing room where her ladyship was sitting, yawning, over the latest lending library novel. He informed her of the name of her visitor. He was pleased that his mistress seemed to welcome the information, directing him to bring Miss Keith to her at once.

When Chloe was seated on a couch near her hostess, she wasted no time in coming to the point.

"A very unpleasant man called Jerold Peke came to visit me in my boarding house tonight. I believe that you know him, and that he has made himself obnoxious to you recently."

Lady Barbara gave an exaggerated shudder, her beautiful little face wrinkling in distaste. "I vow, he's the *horridest* creature, Miss Keith! Cousin Randal was obliged to give him a sharp setdown for presuming to attach himself to me at Lady Merston's ball, and for trying to offer for me without speaking to my papa first."

"He came to me tonight with the intention of levying what the Scots call *blackmail* upon me," announced Chloe. "Since he seeks to involve your happiness and good name in his dastardly plot, I set out at once to warn you, and to tell you exactly what he proposes."

The charming little face beneath the copper curls hardened into a fine maturity. "Yes, please! You must tell me."

Chloe, who had not been too sure what the other girl's response would be, breathed a sigh of relief that there would be neither vapors nor a swoon to contend with. "Peke has got hold of the fact that Lord Randal helped me to escape from my stepbrother, who was trying to rob me and gamble away my money," she began, and then briefly related the whole story of the ride from Smoulton to London, including the purchase of Amigo, in plain unemotional prose.

Lady Barbara seemed to find the tale fascinating, and listened intently. When it was told, she asked, "What is Peke's scheme?"

Chloe drew in a steadying breath. "Sir Jerold told me tonight that he would come to you and tell you that I was—was Lord Randal's mistress," she explained, her cheeks blushing scarlet but her eyes steady on Lady Barbara's.

Unexpectedly Milady giggled. "But that's absurd!"

Chloe's eyebrows rose. "Of course it is, but how did you know?"

"Well, for one thing, I've known Randal since we were in short coats, and he just isn't the kind of man who would—*do that* to a girl like you," she explained.

This comment might not have satisfied a logician, but it brought a warm, sweet smile to Chloe's lips. "No, he isn't, is he? I think he's the kind of man who takes his responsibility toward all women very seriously. Peke said nothing less than truth tonight when he jeered that Lord Randal was a 'perfect knight.' But is that the whole reason you said Peke's charges were absurd?" In the interests of saving the other girl's happiness, Chloe set herself to repeat Reggie's evaluation of herself as a wretched little dab of a girl.

But, eyes sparkling with fun, Milady interrupted,

"Not the *whole* reason, no! You see, I saw you with that gorgeous man in the skirt—"

"Kilt!" begged Chloe in an anguished voice.

Barbara giggled. "So Papa keeps telling me! But you cannot fob me off, Chloe Keith. I saw you looking at him that day we were introduced at Astley's. Mr. Roderick McLeod, is it not? It was immediately plain to me that neither Randal, beautiful as he undoubtedly is, nor any other man, could ever interest *you* as long as your Laird is in the picture."

Chloe had the look of one struck by a blinding revelation. "So *that's* what's been the matter with me," she said softly.

"And with him, too, I have no doubt," added Barbara. "I noticed how anxiously he followed you when you ran away from Peke that day. Och, he's a bonny man, your Hieland laddie!" she teased. "I'd be sighing over Rod McLeod myself, if I hadn't decided to marry Randal Beresford years ago."

"Does Lord Randal know?" smiled Chloe.

"No, I haven't told him yet," the other girl admitted with a laugh. "I wanted the poor fellow to have some freedom before he had to settle down!" Then she added softly, "In view of this latest start of Peke's, perhaps I'll arrange things so Randal decides he'd better marry me to protect me. Oh, he'll think it's his own idea, of course! I wouldn't wish him to know I'd planned the whole."

Chloe regarded the laughing, exquisite little face almost enviously. "I wish I knew how to do it," she confessed. "Every time I talk to Rod, we end up at daggers-drawing."

"You have only to let him think he's the master—the Laird." Chloe thought of Reggie and Sir Jerold and Mr. Wilferd and Amigo's first owner. "I'm not very good at letting men think they're my master," she said, rebelliously. "Most of them aren't as good as I am at handling horses, and they're so patronizing and stubborn and—male!"

"But we wouldn't really want them to be any other way, would we?" asked Lady Barbara, who had known very few men, and most of them her own class. "I have observed that when they are *sure* you think them to be superior, the best of them seem to be willing to admit that we females are fine and precious and worth working and dying for." She sighed romantically. "Is it not pleasant to be cherished?"

Chloe knew she would quarrel or weep if this conversation were to continue. "What is your plan?" she asked.

"I'll announce my engagement to Randal. We aren't engaged; Peke lied to you. Then I'll invite you to be a bridesmaid. Sir Jerold wouldn't dare try to cause a scandal in that situation."

Chloe frowned. "Lady Barbara, thank you, but it is not possible. You can't have looked at me! Little and brown and scrawny and weathered as an old boot—no social graces—no family background! To include me in your wedding party would make you a laughing-stock!" She smiled grimly. "Have you forgotten I'm a circus performer? Only think what Lord Dickson would have to say!"

Lady Barbara considered this seriously. "Then you must stop being a circus performer. You really don't

178

enjoy it for yourself, do you? Randal was telling me that you have this urgent desire to make up to Amigo for his earlier sufferings. This is generous of you, but I do not at all agree that he needs to perform at Astley's. The fun he has with you and the grooms at Kindlewick should surely suffice him. And you, I am convinced, would be the better off, and safer from such persons as Sir Jerold—and *happier*—with your Scottish gentleman, would you not?"

Chloe admitted that all this was true. At Kindlewick she had had everything, she realized: Aunt Janet's love and companionship, a fine place to assemble her stable of horses and start her school, the valuable assistance of Rod—*there was the rub!* By her own willful behavior she had spoiled any chance at a happy relationship with that difficult man. How could she ask him to take her back now, after what she had said and done? Could she bear to humble herself to any man? To plead for another chance to be with him? Her expressive little face darkened with humiliation at the thought. And even more devastating was the idea that he might not care one way or another, whether she returned or stayed away!

"I wish," said Chloe between set teeth, "that I could tell what people were thinking just by looking at them!"

"My papa says he can do so," remarked Lady Barbara, "but I have noticed that he is as often gulled as any other man." She studied the set countenance of the other girl. "Could you bear to tell me why you have need of that ability at this moment?"

But Chloe found she could not tell her charming companion of her demeaning lack of confidence in her own desirability, and her fear that Roderick McLeod had very little interest in her. So she rose to her feet and smiled steadily at Lady Barbara. "Thank you for

179

seeing me, and for sharing your plans with me," she said quietly. "Perhaps you'd better warn Lord Randal of Peke's bitter enmity—put him on his guard against some other vicious attack?"

Lady Barbara agreed. "And you? What will you do now?"

"I shall go back to my boarding house and confide in Aunt Janet, I think. If there is any chance I might return to Kindlewick Farm . . ." her wistful smile brought a sudden sadness to Lady Barbara.

"I am sure they will both welcome you back with open arms," she comforted.

"In any event, I must find out what Sir Jerold is up to. It was cowardly of me to leave Aunt Janet to deal with him alone," Chloe berated herself.

Sped on her way by Milady's kindly assurances of support in her future plans, Chloe left the mansion and climbed into the coach which had been waiting outside. The driver, cold and tired at this late hour, was less than enthusiastic about the distance he would have to cover to restore Chloe to her home, and grumbled that he hoped there'd be a little something extra for his long vigil. Chloe mollified him by promising him a good round sum for his trouble. When he had descended and shut the door after her, the girl huddled in one corner of the musty vehicle and tried to decide on a course of action. Rod's face kept getting in the way, and she could not rid her mind of the memory of the angry things he had said to her.

It was obvious to the girl that she must leave London, thus removing Peke's weapon against Lord Randal. Whether she went to Kindlewick or somewhere else, her first step must be to remove herself from Peke's manipulations. But another thought intruded upon these gloomy meditations. What was her responsibility to Sergeant-Major Astley? He had spent money on posters advertising her appearance with Amigo. What if he insisted that she remain to perform until that outlay was repaid? Could she offer him a small sum to recompense him? After all, the posters had listed other attractions as well as Amigo. The Astleys might not feel that Chloe had any special debt to them. Still, they had given her the chance she had asked for. She owed it to them to give them a little notice, perhaps to perform once more?

She must disappear as soon as possible, that was clear. Then, if Lady Barbara brought Lord Randal to the point of making a declaration, Sir Jerold's guns would be spiked, surely?

But what if Rod utterly refused to take her back? Then perhaps Aunt Janet could find her a small barn or old stable nearby which she could rent, and from which she could conduct her riding school. That way, there might be a chance of seeing a large, unpredictable stern-jawed Scottish landowner from time to time. With this rather mournful image her mind contented itself during the latter part of the ride.

Chapter Fifteen

UNFORTUNATELY FOR THE PLANS of Chloe and Lady Barbara, Sir Jerold had had second thoughts and recruited his friend and evil genius, Mr. Wilferd, to advise him. That wily rogue got the story out of him in a trice, and made short work of his pupil's pretensions.

"Damme, Jerold old man, you've made a bloody mull of this. Why did you not consult me before you approached the girl? She's probably off to warn her protector, and you'll have a duel on your hands before you're a day older."

"That's where you're wrong," countered Peke with a sly grin. "Beresford's out of town today and is not expected back till late tomorrow, by which time I'll have the girl secure."

"And if she decides that the notoriety she'll get from your tale will serve her better in her profession than the doubtful privilege of being your convenient?" jibed his companion.

Sir Jerold frowned, pushing his thin lips out as petulantly as would a small spoiled boy. "How is this?"

"You nodcock, she's a public performer! A scandal linking her to a highly-placed gentleman will bring every dandy and fine lady in London to gape at her and whisper! You've handed her a honey-fall!"

"She did not act as though she thought so," objected Jerold, obstinately.

Wilferd elevated pale blond eyebrows. "Of course not, my dear boy! The little minx knows enough to keep you on the *qui vive!* Now, let us consider this very provocative situation, and see how best you may get both profit and satisfaction from it!"

Thus it happened that Sir Jerold had not appeared at Chloe's boarding house by the time she returned, to be met in the front hallway by a belligerent female duo armed with, respectively, riding crop and rolling pin. She stared at her two champions, open-mouthed. Aunt Janet, not a whit discomfited by Chloe's obvious amazement, condescended to explain.

"We have prepared a warm reception for your would-be ravisher," she announced complacently.

In spite of her deep exhaustion and anxiety, Chloe could not restrain a chuckle. "From your unruffled state, I would guess the creature has not yet made his appearance," she said.

"No, and nor he won't tonight, I should suspect," said their landlady, "since 'tis past midnight. I'll just lock the doors and put out the lamps, and if the dastard comes knocking, me good man will see to him!"

The gentleman thus slightingly referred to did not arrive, however.

The following morning the militant ladies were up and prepareing themselves for any eventuality by eating a good breakfast and positioning their weapons on the hall seat near the front door. For her part, Chloe set out for the Royal Grove to inform the Sergeant-Major of her decision to quit the circus. It would not be an easy interview, for the girl knew how dedicated Astley was to his establishment, and not only because of the money he was making. He had the true flair of the entrepreneur as well as the skills of a horseman.

Astley's cheerful, brick-red countenance fell as he listened to her apologetic little speech. Before she had finished talking, he broke in, "But this is being foolish beyond permission, as the nobs like to say! You and Amigo are in the way of being a great success—a truly Stellar Attraction! It isn't just his feats of skill, for you must know," and he bent a kindly eye upon the unhappy girl, "I've many horses better trained and able to perform more daring feats than he is capable of! It's his comic way that sets the company to laughing. They love him—and it's plain he loves being the clown."

Chloe squared her shoulders and faced him resolutely. "I am more than conscious of your kindness and the opportunity you have given Amigo and me," she said in her clear little voice. "And so perhaps I shall tell you that I have been approached by a nobleman who wishes to . . . to—" blushing hotly, Chloe was unable to continue.

Astley drew in a deep breath of anger which actually caused his chest to swell alarmingly. "You should let Mrs. Astley or myself know if you are being bothered! Just tell the fine lordling that you are under our protection, and that I'll see him in—that is, I'll take steps to protect you from molestation!"

"It is not altogether physical harm this man threatens," said Chloe. "He has a plan to blackmail a man who has been a good friend to me, if I do not agree to his demands. The situation is so insupportable that I know the only way out of it with any credit is to disappear—which I have planned to do as soon as possible."

Astley considered her, frowning. "Well, child, I suppose you know your own business best, but it will be a loss to the Royal Grove—I admit it! When do you wish to go?"

"I had thought I might stay at least until after tomorrow night's performance, which you had already advertised," said the girl. "That way, your customers would not be done out of any of the exhibitions you have promised them—"

"That is excellent!" boomed Astley, clapping her on the shoulder hearteningly. "And I must tell you that I have been giving your performance some thought, and have come upon an idea which will make your final appearance a notable one! Let me show you," and he took her arm and led her out toward the hurdle and water tank in the center of the circus.

As they came nearer, Chloe discovered that a huge wooden hoop had been affixed to the hurdle Amigo was to jump over. "This will be covered with thin paper," explained Astley. "You will guide Amigo through it. You will wish to practice today, and perhaps again tomorrow, to show him what he is expected to do." Then, noting her worried look, he said with bluff good humor, "He will do it, child! Just let him get the hang of it, and all's bowmon, as they say! Come, try it out! It will have its first paper cover by the time you've saddled Amigo."

Touched with a faint, undefinable sense of alarm which she attributed to the thought of Amigo's being frightened or hurt by the new trick, Chloe went off to the stables to fetch her stallion. There the grooms informed her that Astley, whose fondness of pyrotechnics was well known, had secured a new lot, called

185

starbursts, which he intended setting off just after Amigo made his triumphant leap through the paper-covered hoop. For some reason, the knowledge of this new ploy served to increase Chloe's uneasiness. What if Amigo became frightened by the unaccustomed flares of light? Then her sober common sense came into play. The fireworks would not be set off until after the stallion had cleared the hurdle, so they could hardly distract him from the jump. So reassuring herself, she mounted the eager horse and rode him to the center ring of the circus.

While Chloe was familiarizing Amigo with the dangers and delights of his new act, Sir Peter Daley was arriving at the elegant townhouse of his long-time friend Lord Randal Beresford. Ushered into the breakfast parlor, where his lordship was morosely partaking of a modest repast, Sir Peter greeted his host with a cheeriness which Lord Randal seemed to find repulsive.

"Thought you was coming to stay with me for the weekend," Sir Peter explained, seating himself and waving an encouraging hand to the butler, an old ally of his who was officiating at the sideboard. "Yes, I'll have a taste of everything, Bates. Ridden in from Greenleaves, and I'm sharp set." He focused his attention upon his friend. "When you didn't arrive by midnight, I thought I'd mistaken the day—or perhaps it was I who was to have come to you?"

Randal frowned. "Sorry! I'd forgotten I had been promised to you for the weekend," he acknowledged. "Got things on my mind," he muttered, and drained his coffee cup.

Sir Peter surveyed the well-laden plate Bates was offering him, "Thank you! Very appetizing! Yes, coffee will do nicely." He faced his host. "Well, if I wasn't mistaken, what was it that prevented you from coming to Greenleaves?" He scanned his friend's face carefully. "Dyspeptic, old boy? Or a new Incognita?"

Lord Randal groaned. "Would it were something so easily dealt with! No, it's that ridiculous chit Chloe. She's got herself into another scrape. What a ninny-hammer! It seems she cannot go on by herself for two days running without falling into some new folly! The latest start is to get herself advertised all over town as a clown at Astley's."

Sir Peter goggled. "A clown?" he searched his memory. "Chloe? Isn't she the one who wishes to start a riding school?"

"The same," said Lord Randal grimly. "I thought I had her safely settled at Kindlewick Farm, and in the way of being a success with her school—for there's no doubt the chit can ride, and what's more, can teach children. And now what do we see? Astley's! Trick riding! *Clowns!*"

Sir Peter knew it was incumbent upon any friend of Lord Randal's to offer help, but he was not exactly sure what form of assistance might be acceptable. "Shouldn't think you would need to concern yourself at this point, Randal," he ventured. "After all, the chit is of age, and has an older woman to advise her, you told me—"

It was immediately obvious this was not the counsel Lord Randal was seeking. "In the first place," he began ominously, "I shall be best pleased if you do not call Chloe 'the chit'—"

"But you did so yourself, twice, just now!" protested Peter.

"That," said Randal (his friend thought a trifle pompously), "is different. And as for an older woman to advise her—! It appears this aunt of McLeod's has not only permitted Chloe's outlandish behavior, she has

187

actually contributed to it! She is aiding and abetting the ch—the child by residing with her near the Royal Grove."

"But surely her presence with the—er—child is a guarantee of proper chaperonage?"

" 'Proper'?" challenged Randal fiercely. "While she permits Chloe to display herself daily—and I have no doubt, nightly!—on that ridiculous beast! She will catch her death from such frequent plunges into cold water!"

Sir Peter, faint but willing, tried to make sense out of his friend's impassioned tirade. "I believe the Royal Grove seldom offers two performances a day," he began in an extenuating tone.

Lôrd Randal's bitterness was not assuaged. "What has that to say to anything?"

"Well, you *said* she was appearing twice daily—" he began.

"That she should appear even once is an affront to decency!" snapped Randal.

"What are you proposing to do about it?" asked his friend, goaded into challenge.

"Ha!" retorted Lord Randal darkly.

Sir Peter did not consider this much of an answer. It is possible the two friends might have fallen into an argument, if Bates had not appeared at this exact moment with the announcement that Sir Jerold Peke and Mr. Wilferd were at the door, requesting an interview with Lord Randal.

This intelligence, which his friend feared would put the cap sheaf upon Lord Randal's ill-humor, seemed on the contrary to afford him intense pleasure.

"Do they indeed!" he said trenchantly, with what Bates in the servants' hall later characterized as quite a nasty smile. "By all means show them into the library, where I shall be ready to receive them!"

Sir Peter could not like this decision. "You are forever saying you cannot endure either of them, calling them trumped-up mushrooms, and blacklegs, and I know not what else! Why should you waste your time upon them now, when we have other matters to deal with?"

But Lord Randal, paying no attention to what was, in this case at least, a wiser head, strode out into the hallway and across to the library, where he took up his stand on the hearth rug beneath the rather grim-looking picture of his parent which had been painted by Sir Joshua Reynolds and was thought to be one of his better efforts. Randal gestured the nervously hovering Sir Peter to a chair beside the hearth. Thus suitably seconded, Milord waited for his uninvited guests.

Sir Peter did not count himself a great brain, and, among his friends, was generally regarded as a bit of a slow-top, if a deuced fine fellow, but even his limited perceptions informed him that the smiling visitors were up to no good. When Bates had closed the library door behind them, they advanced into the room and greeted their host with every appearance of bluff good humor. Lord Randal's face was as grim as his pictured sire's, and he did not offer his hand.

"To what am I indebted for the—uh—pleasure of this visit?" he asked, with an icy civility which was in itself an insult. There was a sneer on his lips which Sir Peter could not like, so menacing and provocative it seemed.

Sir Jerold, whose narrow pallid face had flushed a deep red at Lord Randal's refusal to shake hands, and at the absence of an offer that the visitors be seated, struggled to maintain his aplomb. He glanced meaningfully at Sir Peter.

"Since the business on which we have come, Beresford, is of a particularly private nature, you might wish to excuse Sir Peter—"

"I have no business, either private or otherwise, with you, sir," said Lord Randal with what his friend recognized as deliberate provocation.

"Now, now, perhaps we should not be hasty, Milord," Mr. Wilferd interposed with his inane laugh.

"Why not?" drawled Lord Randal insultingly. "The less time I am compelled to breathe the air Peke pollutes, the better."

Even the complacent Wilferd went white at this studied insolence, while Sir Jerold surged forward with his hands out like claws to seize this tormentor.

"Jerold!" warned his friend, but the damage was done. Instead of retreating from the attack, Lord Randal stepped into it, and the enraged Peke found his hand in sudden contact with Milord's face. His fingernails caught against Lord Randal's cheek, and a shallow gash resulted, marked by the flow of a small quantity of blood.

"Ah!" breathed Milord with satisfaction, his fingers touching the moisture on his cheek.

Wilferd was looking shocked and Peke appalled at this development. Sir Jerold drew back hastily, and began to stammer something about an accident, and his demmed hot temper, but Lord Randal would have none of his apologies.

"I am the injured party, I believe," he said smoothly. "My seconds will wait upon you tomorrow. And not pistols, I think? It is so fatally easy to have a—friend concealed in the shrubbery with an extra weapon." And he maintained his wide, mirthless smile until the stunned duo had made their way out of his house.

There was a pregnant silence in the library after they left. Then Sir Peter drew the first real breath he'd taken in several minutes. "Feeling quite the thing, old boy?" he inquired with massive sarcasm. When his friend did not answer, Peter went on in rising anger, "I knew you had this odd kick in your gallop, Ran, but by Heaven! this is too much! Have you run mad?"

"I wish to remove this carrion from the face of the earth," said Lord Randal. "He struck Chloe in the face, you know."

Sir Peter was shocked. "In that case, something should be done. But a duel? That honors the fellow above his worth."

"Would you have me hire a brace of bullies to mill him down?" snapped Lord Randal.

"Have you thought what the *Ton* will be saying?" When his friend made no reply, Sir Peter said anxiously, "You should have heard the fellow out! We would have had an inkling of what villainy he was up to!"

Milord shrugged. "He was up to blackmail—and no, I don't know what he had in mind, particularly! Does such a creature need facts? He invents them as he goes!"

"Well, I intend to circulate a few rumors myself!" announced Sir Peter stoutly. "I'll drop in at White's and The Strand and even Almack's, and tell a few trusted friends that the upstart Peke struck you in the face and is to be punished for it."

Lord Randal looked up sharply, frowning, and then his eyes grew intent. After a moment he began to grin. "That's the barber!" he said. "Be sure to explain exactly what *I* said to *him,* to invite the blow. Once that story gets around, no one will be interested in whatever lies Peke had intended to spread. Anything he tries to allege will be considered mere spite in reprisal."

Sir Peter nodded, grinning. "The fellow will have to leave London! I'll recruit Ashdean as the other second. He's the best man with a sword outside the salon masters."

"Swords! My father insisted I learn to fence, and I've

191

played at it when I was up at Cambridge, but I'm no duellist!"

"I don't suppose Peke is either, come to that," advised Sir Peter. "Can't see our blustering Sir Jerold facing cold steel very cheerfully. Well, if not pistols and not swords, what had you considered?"

"I'd like to horsewhip the fellow," said Milord, grimly.

"You don't need seconds for that," objected Sir Peter. "It would make a laughing-stock of both of you."

"I have it!" grinned Lord Randal. "Lances—on horseback—until one of us is knocked down! Peke's forever going on about what a bruising rider he is, so he wouldn't dare to cry off!"

Sir Peter considered the idea, then shook his head. "It's irregular. Freakish. And you could be seriously injured."

"Oh, we'd wear padded breastplates," Lord Randal shrugged.

Sir Peter regarded him shrewdly. "I don't think our windy friend will come up to scratch," he said slowly. "I think he'll suddenly discover urgent business on the Continent."

"So much the better. In that case, I'd deserve a vote of thanks from the Beau Monde for ridding it of such a Captain Hackum." He raised worried eyes to his friend. "I only hope he will not try to put pressure on Chloe now he finds himself at *point non plus* with me."

"Perhaps we'd better drop in at Astley's and have a word with the girl, before I start my rumor-mongering in the clubs?"

"I'll do it myself," began Milord, but his friend shook his head firmly.

"We must avoid the very appearance of evil," Sir Peter cautioned. "No use giving fuel to Peke's innuendoes."

"That's a fine pious mouthful," groused Lord Randal, but was enough struck with his friend's warning to agree to wait for Sir Peter to finish his spreading of rumor before setting off with him for the Royal Grove that evening to discover the whereabouts of Chloe's lodgings.

Peke had scarcely waited to get inside Mr. Wilferd's coach before turning on his mentor. "A damned dangerous mess you've gotten me into, you smatterer!" he began, glaring at the other man. "A duel!"

"Oh, you'll get out of it some way," sneered Wilferd. "You always do, when the man's anything but a green youth—"

"That's a lie!" snarled Sir Jerold.

"Oh, take a damper," urged his companion. "You'd better recollect some pressing business in Italy, or Greece, or perhaps China! Take a vacation for a few months until this blows over."

"I'll spread the story we planned to threaten him with—then maybe I won't have to go," began Peke.

"Who will believe you, once this latest *on dit* makes the rounds?" said Wilferd coldly. "Do you imagine for one moment that it won't get about? Daley is going to tell everyone that Beresford said you polluted the air—and you scratched his face!"

Sir Jerold began cursing in a monotone. Wilferd watched him with assessing eyes. Then he shrugged lightly.

"I'll deliver you at your chambers, Jerold," he said.

"Who shall we get to act with you as my second?"

"You aren't serious," stated Wilferd. "But if you are, you'll need two. I find I shall be too busy to act for you."

Peke stared at him in the dim light within the carriage, his mouth open.

"I find you boring, and bad *ton*," Wilferd continued. "I can't think why I bothered with you so long." The carriage drew up before Peke's chambers. "Good-bye, Jerold. Don't bother to look me up."

Peke made no move to get out. "You don't mean that!"

Wilferd uttered his inane, mirthless laugh. "Oh, don't I? You're finished, Jerold, and I never back a loser."

"I'm finished, am I? Perhaps Beresford will find out differently! And you, too!"

He swung down from the carriage and rushed into the building. Cursing him, Wilferd hung out of the vehicle and grasped the door to swing it closed. His coachman touched the horses and they paced off down the street.

Chapter Sixteen

THE LANDLADY'S SON set out very early for Kindle-wick Farm on Sunday morning, but from having lingered to watch a brawl in London, and lost his way once after he left the metropolis, and above all, from having the greatest slug in nature to ride on (as he complained to Mr. Roderick McLeod), he did not arrive at the farm until late in the afternoon. When he had delivered his message to its master, he was taken to the kitchen and treated to a satisfying repast while the Laird scanned Janet's letter with ever increasing alarm and annoyance.

What had they gotten themselves into? Hadn't he warned the silly females? Hadn't he told Janet there were hazards in the city which two blunderheaded women were not prepared, by training or experience, to deal with? Oh, yes, fumed Rod, he had told them, but when did women ever listen to the sensible advice of men who cared what happened to them? No, they went off blithely disregarding the counsel of wiser heads than their own! And now they see what has come of it! He shook the pages of Janet's neat handwriting, wishing he had someone's shoulders under his fingers rather than the insensate paper.

Luckily, he could leave for London within the hour. He had matters at Kindlewick in hand; the laborers were beginning to get the new dwellings built for the crofters who were coming down with their families from Scotland. It was as well he had gone with Cameron back to the Towers, that uncomfortable, cold, badly rundown stone building which had been home to his ancestors for several hundred years. The last of Torquil McLeod's descendants were pitifully glad to see the young Laird, and looked to him to mend their fortunes. They were mostly older folk, since the young men had gone off—or been sent as laborers after The Trouble—to the New World. Rod himself had taken the best of the young men south with him to England, to work as crofters near Kindlewick. Now he addressed the whole remnant of Torquil McLeod's clan, gathered at the Towers to offer the new Laird their fealty.

"I am established in England," he told them, after the brief moving ceremony was ended. "I offer you two choices. You may come back there with me, and receive new, fertile holdings, or become part of the staff of my household and estate there. Or you may offer your loyalty to the Laird of the other McLeod clan."

There were murmurs of anger and distress. Rod checked them sharply. "The founder of our line had two sons, as well you know. The elder, Norman, seems to have been a stronger and wiser man than his brother, and his line flourished. Whereas our progenitor, Torquil, bequeathed us little but strife and dissension, even within our own ranks. With the result that the Clan McLeod of Norman's blood has flourished, while our own fortunes have steadily declined. Until now. I have planned a new way for myself, and I'll accept as many of you as wish to join me in England. As for those who do not choose to leave Scotland, I'll enter negotiations with the other McLeod to have you join his sept, and give each of you a gift so you will not have to go to him penniless."

But they had all chosen to follow the young Laird into exile in England, and were on their way now, under the guidance of Matt and Cameron. Rod sighed. He hoped the older ones would not be too wretched in their fine new homes. If only Aunt Janet were here to help him settle them in! Her brisk good sense and pawky humor were just what was needed. Well now, perhaps—if this folly of the performing horse was done with—

He folded Janet's letter neatly. Then he went upstairs to bathe and dress in town clothes, first sending a maid to inform Alan he was to accompany his master to the city in half an hour. Alan had already constituted himself the Laird's ghillie, and Rod had not had the heart to discourage him, although his delighted, ceremonious hovering was sometimes hard to bear.

It was dusk when they reached London, and they racked up at McLeod's Hotel, to receive such an impressive welcome that the regular guests were whispering among themselves. After eating the formal dinner his host insisted upon serving, Rod lost no more time in seeking out the boarding house in which Aunt Janet and her troublesome protegee were living. He had no trouble, for he had made sure to get its direction from the boy who brought Aunt Janet's letter.

He was surprised at the reception he received. When he had knocked, he requested of the formidable creature who swung open the door that she inform Miss McLeod that she had a visitor.

The woman reached to the table nearby and picked up a rolling pin, inquiring belligerently what he thought he was up to?

"I am *up to* seeing my aunt, Miss Janet McLeod, if you will be good enough to inform her that her nephew Roderick is here, at her urgent request, I may add!"

A beaming smile transformed the Amazon's countenance.

"Oh, ye're the Laird!" she cried, hastily disposing of the rolling pin and bobbing an awkward curtsy. "Be pleased to come in, yer Lordship—Lairdship—well, I'm sure I don't know the proper way to call you, sir—"

"Mr. McLeod will do very nicely," said Rod, with a wide smile of irrepressible amusement.

The landlady was an instant conquest.

"Miss McLeod and I agreed to set up a watch against that creature who tried to flummery Miss Chloe. I'm that glad you came, sir, for the girl is like a babe unborn in this great city—not up to the knocker, as you might say! But there now! No loose-screw is going to give the child a slip on the shoulder while Maggie Beamish is here to stop it!"

Rod moved into the hallway and took her hand in his big one. "I thank you, Mrs. Beamish," he said with formal courtesy. "It is indeed a great relief to me to know that such a good woman as yourself has been protecting the child. I have come to take her back where she belongs. Now if you will show me to my aunt—?"

"Well, that I can't, exactly, sir, at this minute, since Miss McLeod is out at the apothecary's picking up some potion for Miss Chloe."

"She is ill?" asked Rod sharply.

" 'Tis a mere phlegmatic humor of the nose," pronounced the good woman. "Comes of falling into that trough of water last night. Drenched and dripping, she was, when that creature brought her home."

"There will be no more of that, I promise you," said Rod, between his teeth. "Is Miss Chloe laid upon her bed? Perhaps you had better accompany me to their rooms."

"Oh, yes, I'll be glad to, sir! Very proper!" agreed the landlady, bustling off up the stairs ahead of him. "This way, Mr. McLeod, sir!"

So it was that Chloe, feeling miserable with a snuffly cold in the head, was suddenly presented with the living, breathing original of all her lonely dreams—and sneezed so violently that her head snapped back against the headboard with a dull thud.

And of course Rod laughed.

She looked so tiny, so wretched with her little nose red and her huge eyes dark-shadowed in her small face, that he might have been forgiven for his amusement. Miss Keith, however, had no intention of forgiving such insensitivity as would make mock of a person laid low upon a bed of suffering. In a perhaps natural desire to avenge herself for Rod's laughter, the girl said coldly, "What are *you* doing here?" in far from welcoming tones.

Rod compounded his offense by taking a very bossy attitude.

"I've come," he stated, unwisely, "to put an end to this absurd charade and get you and Aunt Janet back where you belong before you kill yourself or shame us all."

In view of the fact that she had just retired from a promising career at Astley's for purely altruistic reasons, this arrogant announcement could not do other than offend Chloe's already lacerated sensibilities. The presence of the fascinated landlady put somewhat of a restraint upon her tongue, but she managed to say, indignantly, "Since my name is not the same as yours, and no one will know of any connection between us if you do not tell them, I cannot see how any behavior of mine could ever bring shame upon you!"

Rod also was conscious of the eyes and ears of the landlady, and heartily wished he had not so meticulously observed the conventions as to insist upon her presence at a confrontation of so personal a nature. He was of two minds whether to try to continue it under the interested surveillance of the woman, or to retire to the hallway and wait for Janet's return. She at least would have the decency to let him settle matters with this enraging child in private. Or would she? While these thoughts were racing through his head, the door from the hallway opened and his aunt entered the sickroom.

"Thank God you have come!" burst from the harassed man, rushing blindly upon his fate. "This little limmer willna listen to reason, and insists upon defying those who know better than she what is good for her!"

"What is a *limmer?*" croaked Chloe, eyes bright with rage.

"'T means a rogue or scoundrel," advised Janet, adding el to the fire.

This answer pleased neither of the combatants. Rod cast his aunt a look of reproach, while Chloe turned a blazing glare upon the laird.

"You *know* I meant it as—as a term of endearment," ground out the man, his cheeks dark red with embarrassment, and sweat beginning to break out upon his tanned forehead.

Janet observed these signs with satisfaction, but Chloe was not as well aware of male reactions as Rod's aunt.

"Endearment!" she fairly shrieked. "I knew you were a cold, arrogant, suspicious, unfeeling *man,* but I did not dream you would call me a—a *scoundrel!"* She sneezed violently again, rather spoiling the effect of

her peroration. Blowing her nose heartily, she added, in rather muffled accents, "I'll stay at Astley's as long as I wish, and take part in as many absurd charades as I can, and—and I do not wish to see your cold sneering face ever again!"

Rod's face had indeed assumed a look of frozen arrogance. He made Chloe a formal bow. "If that is the way you wish it, Miss Keith—?"

"It is!" snapped the wretched girl, already regretting her folly but too stubborn to admit it in front of witnesses.

"Very well then. I shall remove my offensive presence and cease to annoy you with my unwanted advice. I wish you well in your new—*career*—and always!"

Chloe thought that she had seen nothing more devastating than the rear view of those broad, dependable, attractive shoulders as they moved out of sight. With a small, almost silent wail of grief and exasperation she threw herself into her pillows and began to cry.

Aunt Janet motioned the landlady out of the room and began calmly to unwrap her purchases. "Now, my dear child, since you have routed that arrogant man, let us get you in shape for the continuation of your lifelong career at Astley's. The next performance is tomorrow, you know, and you'll have to be there early in order to rehearse Amigo in that dangerous new trick."

"Oh, Aunt Janet, what have I done?" sobbed the girl.

"Just exactly as you ought," soothed the woman, taking the shaking girl into her motherly arms.

The Laird, getting himself out of the boarding house as quickly as he was able, felt no such sense of reassurance. He was beginning to think he had made a serious mull of the business, and to blame his aunt for her indiscretion in answering the question which set off the brangle. *"Women! There is no living with them!"* he concluded, as several other men had done in like case before him. Then he was forced to admit that he had perhaps been less than diplomatic himself, and that his really sincere and compassionate desire to protect the girl had not been phrased with just the delicacy and persuasiveness someone like Lord Randal might have given it. What with Alan obviously bursting with curiosity on the one hand, and his own increasing desire to go back and beg the chit's pardon on the other, he was in a highly uncomfortable state as he rode back to McLeod's Hotel. By the time he got there, it was very late indeed, and he knew there was nothing more he could do that night. However, he left a call—unnecessary, as it later happened—to be called very early, and went to bed full of noble resolves to forgive the girl and make all right on the morrow.

In the event, after a completely sleepless night, he was able to present himself at the boarding house at an unfashionably early hour, only to meet with the intelligence that Miss Keith had already left for Astley's, but that his aunt was waiting to speak with him in her private parlor. Thankful for small mercies, he mounted the stairs, very conscious of the landlady's interested gaze on his neck.

Aunt Janet received him with a deep formal curtsy.

"What nonsense is this?" he snapped, and moved forward to give her the accustomed hug.

The woman smiled up at him and kissed his cheek lightly, as was her wont.

"I wasn't sure whether my affection would be welcome, after yesterday," she said provocatively.

"Aunt Janet!" warned her nephew. "I know I made a mull of it with Chloe—"

"Indeed you did," his aunt agreed cordially. "Of all

the silly gowks! Have you not learned how to handle us yet—ye stupid limmer?"

"How *could you?*" her nephew protested. "Ye ken verra weel it doesn't mean 'scoundrel' when it's used from one friend to another!"

"But then you weren't behaving in a very friendly manner, from all I was able to observe," reminded his aunt.

Rod groaned. "I canna think what gets into me when I talk with the wee lass," he confessed. "Everything she says seems to put my back up!"

"Could it be that you are still holding what her stepbrother told you against her? Do you doubt her virtue, or her moral sense?"

"Janet!" snapped her nephew in outrage.

"That's what you've given the child to think," Janet told him.

"But I *told* her—"

"*What* did you tell her?"

"Not to forget who was the Laird," Rod said, low-voiced.

"Oh, very ardent and lover-like!" Janet shook her head. "I'm surprised the child wasn't able to read a whole declaration in form from those significant words! Crystal clear! Everything but the date named!"

Rod pokered up. "I had always been given to understand that females grasped these things very quickly—if they wished to do so."

"Not by me were you given to understand any such nonsense! I am out of patience with you, Roderick. Here's the girl given in her notice, to save Beresford any embarrassment, and you—"

It was the wrong thing to have said. At mention of Beresford's name, Rod's face assumed its closed, arrogant—or as Janet now characterized it—his stubborn look. "I see! She would not quit the silly ploy for my sake, but she would drop everything at the hint of an awkardness for Lord Randal! I see which way the wind is blowing, and I'm grateful to you for hinting me off!"

"But I haven't hinted . . . explained anything!" wailed Janet, realizing too late what she had done. "That creature Peke's been pestering her, and threatening to blacken Beresford's name, and offering her a *carte blanche—*"

"Very pretty goings-on." Rod was furious; she had known him from a child and could read his expression all too clearly. His smile was arctic. "I thought that had been your purpose in being here—to protect her from such advances! Perhaps she does not wish to be protected! It is all a trick to catch Beresford's attention." And before the indignant woman could utter a syllable, Rod had sketched her a bow and walked out, closing the door firmly after him.

"Damn!" said Janet McLeod.

As Rod mounted his horse outside the boarding house, he was resolving bitterly to return to Kindlewick without delay, and to put all thoughts of females firmly behind him. By the time he had ridden back to the hotel, however, his thoughts had taken a more flexible tone, and he was able to find any number of reasons why he should remain in the metropolis for at least one day. Upon being informed of this, Alan proved his worth as a ghillie by suggesting that they attend the performance at Astley's while they were this close. The Laird seemed much struck by this idea, but sternly commanded his servant not to inform his aunt or anyone else of the projected visit. The Laird then went morosely off to his tailor and ordered three new coats, all in the latest cry, from that delighted man, who vowed it was a sheer pleasure to make for Mr. McLeod, who never needed padding to bring his shoulders into proper balance with his torso. Grunting disparagement of this fulsome praise, Mr. McLeod went on his way.

At that very moment the Lady Barbara, looking enchantingly pretty in an apricot muslin dress with a bronze velvet trim exactly to the color of her artfully tumbled curls, was deciding What To Do about Lord Randal. She had known he was the only man for her the first time she saw him. That he was twelve and she eight years old when they met made no difference. The occasion of this significant encounter was her birthday, and the scene was the elegant Folly in the grounds of Lord Dickson's London home.

Lady Dickson, a willowy beauty much given to the vapors, had instructed the housekeeper and Barbara's governess that the party for her daughter should take place at a comfortable remove from her own person. "I do not wish to see any of the children, and most particularly I do not wish to *hear* them! You will take care of this, Miss Englebert."

So the tempting food was spread, picnic-fashion, on a table in the vine-draped arbor, and the efficient Miss Englebert organized games for the children of the Dickson's circle of friends. The oldest guests were a scornful pair of twins, Gervais and Gloria Chace, and the youngest child was Barbara, even at that age distractingly pretty with her shining red-gold curls and sparkling blue eyes. Gervais, a hulking lad of fifteen, seemed to find the tiny girl's appearance very much to his taste, and while Miss Englebert was busy supervising the games, he made several remarks Barbara was fortunately too young to understand.

Nearly all the children had been deposited with Miss

Englebert by their respective governesses or nannies when Little Lady Barbara raised her eyes to watch the approach of a tall, sturdy boy with thick, shining dark hair above a square, well-featured face. Dark brows and thick black eyelashes emphasized the steadiest gray eyes she had ever seen. He seemed to be a general favorite with the older children, although the Chace twins greeted him coldly. Miss Englebert presented him to his young hostess.

"Lady Barbara, this is Lord Randal Beresford."

Gravely Randal offered her a neatly-wrapped package. Unlike most of the other young guests, who were now clustering greedily at the buffet, Randal stood smiling at his small hostess as she unwrapped his gift. A tiny golden locket engraved with a "B" glowed in the sunlight.

"It is beautiful." Lady Barbara smiled shyly up at the big boy. "I thank you, Randal."

"I am glad you like it," he said. "My mother helped me choose it."

To Barbara, whose mother had never helped her choose anything, this was an even greater wonder than the gift itself.

"Please thank her for me," she said softly.

Randal chuckled. "You are a funny little thing! Here, let me put it on for you. You might have difficulty with the clasp."

Standing very still as the boy's fingers moved at her nape, Barbara felt a new emotion—more than the gratitude and affection she felt for her father and Miss Englebert. Then, breaking into this enchanted moment, there occurred the other incident she could never forget—the incident which brought her eighth birthday party to a disastrous conclusion. The Chace boy strolled over to the pair and took a lounging stance beside Barbara.

"I forgot to give you your whacks," he grinned. There was a smear of chocolate on his mouth.

"Whacks?" the little girl stared up at him, puzzled.

"A birthday spanking—eight whacks and one to grow on."

Randal noted the slight gesture of alarm from the child.

"Chace is joking, of course," he said firmly. "That custom is for boys, not little girls." Although the words were quietly spoken, there was a definite warning in them for the larger youth.

"Who's going to stop me?" challenged Gervais belligerently. Then, observing Randal's steady stare and clenched fists, he backed down. "You've given me a better idea, Beresford." He lunged forward, seized Barbara by the shoulders and kissed her hard.

The next instant he was pulled away from the girl and knocked sprawling on the grass. Until they were separated by a hastily summoned footman, the unevenly matched assailants fought fiercely. Randal's eye was darkened, but he drew Gervais's cork with a satisfactory display of the claret.

Recalling the incident, Lady Barbara's expression became tender. Then gradually a naughty smile parted her lips. *Of course!* Man and boy, Lord Randal could never resist the appeal of a damsel in distress! Lady Barbara went to her escritoire, drew out a sheet of her monogrammed paper, and, with frequent pauses for reflection and a reprehensible chuckle or two, wrote Milord a letter.

At the very moment that Mr. McLeod was purchasing six new neck-cloths, with a grim desire to out-mode the modish Lord Randal, and Lady Barbara was sealing her letter to the same gentleman, Chloe was leaving for the Royal Grove, against all advice and pleading from Janet. "It is my last appearance," the girl said. "I promised Mr. Astley—and I promised Amigo."

"But you are ill!" protested the older woman.

"Pooh! I have worked at Uncle Ned's when I felt far worse than I do now. Believe me, Aunt Janet, I'm much better—and it's just the once more. After tonight . . ." and her voice failed her at the thought. She had burnt her bridges—there would be no going back to Kindlewick now. Putting such agonizing thoughts firmly out of mind, the girl dressed warmly and trudged over to the Royal Grove, where Amigo waited restlessly for her to practice the new trick with him.

He had taken to it well, seeming to enjoy the blind leap at the paper-covered hoop, and the tearing sound as he went through and over the water-filled trough on the other side, now safely covered with the straw mattresses. For even Chloe was not enough of a dedicated performer to wish to immerse herself over and over in cold water when she was suffering from a congestion of the head.

Now she led Amigo to the hurdle, pointed out the trough and mattresses, tore a tiny bit of the paper covering over the hoop, and explained again that they would do what they had been practicing the day before. Amigo seemed to have it all clear in his clever head, and nodded encouragement.

The day was filled with successful practice, and the stableboy who was delegated to recover the huge hoop with paper was getting heartily sick of his task before Chloe called a halt.

"That's it until tonight," she advised him. "Amigo has it clearly in his mind what he's to do. He won't shy at it."

" 'E's a wonder, that 'orse is," the boy nodded. "A reg'ler Sergeant-Major!"

It was approaching the hour for the performance, and Astley's men were setting up the mounts for the fireworks display. Someone would be hidden beside the trough, to set a light to the star-bursts just after Amigo completed his leap. The grooms assured her it would make a dazzling finale for her act.

Chloe walked wearily back to the boarding house to rest before she had to dress herself for the show. Aunt Janet and the landlady had prepared an especially tempting meal, but, what with one thing and another, Chloe could hardly manage more than a few bites. Afterward, she laid herself down on her bed and tried to make her mind a blank. After an hour of this fruitless exercise, she rose even more wearily and dressed for the last time in her gaudy costume.

Aunt Janet accompanied her to the Royal Grove, and took a seat among the early arrivals while Chloe went to the stables to collect Amigo.

Aunt Janet looked around, but was unable to see her nephew, for the very good reason that he was carefully concealing himself at the rear of the covered seats. The show began, and proceeded with all the *élan* and charm for which Astley's troupe was famous. Eventually it was Chloe's turn to lead Amigo into the ring, and the knowledgeable in the audience whispered to their companions to *watch this! A very amusing act!*

It might almost be inferred that Amigo knew this was his final appearance, his swan song. Never had he cavorted so spiritedly; never had so huge an animal presented such a picture of apprehension and alarm. The audience was giggling and guffawing before he had even come to his leap over the hurdle. Chloe, feeling very warm and a little lightheaded, gave him the command to gallop to the hurdle, and endeavored to hold herself straight in the saddle. The great horse pounded down toward the hurdle, and it is safe to say that every eye under the painted roof of the Royal Grove was fixed upon his progress. Many noted for the first time the gigantic hoop with its blind paper cover which was fixed upon the hurdle. Amigo gathered himself for the leap—and then the paper hoop glowed and burst into flame—and Amigo, with a shrill neigh, flew at it, burst through, and landed successfully beyond the filled trough at the other side.

Chloe too maintained her self-possession. She threw her arms up and toppled into the pool as they had practiced. But the pool itself was alight with glancing small flames, and she went under into the cool waters with a shock of relief mingled with the fright. What new ploy of the Sergeant-Major's was this? She had understood that the fireworks were not to begin until after she and Amigo were safely over! Holding her breath, the girl mentally shrugged. At least Amigo had not been startled into forgetting his drill. She wondered how long the flames above her on the surface of the water would burn, and just what she was expected to do? Her lungful of air wouldn't last forever, she thought, with rising anger. Nor would any horse dare the small flames to pull her out of the trough!

The audience was confused but pleasingly alarmed by the unexpected fire. Then, when the fireworks went off, exactly as Astley had planned, they relaxed and told each other it was just one of Astley's brilliant displays, and settled back to await the expected rescue.

But Janet, sitting frozen in her front seat, and Rod McLeod, horrified in the rear row, knew very well that no such dangerous folly would be permitted. Rod was up and out of his chair before anyone else had fully reacted to the sight of the flaming trough. He leaped down the stairs two at a time, and vaulted the waist-high barrier onto the tanbark while Astley and his crew were still staring, rooted at the spectacle.

210

But there was one who was even quicker. Amigo, shivering with alarm and fear of the flames, had trotted back to the trough to rescue his mistress, as he had been trained. He did not see her thrusting her reinforced collar up for his grasp, and he whinnied with nervous excitement. The flames crackled, flying bits of burning paper flew from the charred wooden hoop; the crowd began to cry out. A woman screamed.

Amigo reared and thundered out his challenge. Then he plunged his great head through the flames to the place where Chloe usually waited.

The girl saw and felt the splash of his arrival. Reaching up her arms, she grasped the bridle, lost it, clung to it and let the great head help her to rise and jump out of the trough. Amigo was too overset to continue their routine. His eye had caught a flurry of movement as a man crawled out of concealment between the trough and the framework. This scurrying figure tried to escape across the tanbark to mingle with the rush of men from the sides of the arena. Amigo, beside himself with fear and rage, saw the furtive effort to escape and, plunging in pursuit, reared and lashed downward with his great hooves. Twice he savaged the arsonist before Astley and two grooms got him away.

A cheer went up as Rod picked the bedraggled Chloe from the tanbark where Amigo had dropped her. The girl hardly recognized him. Her anxious gaze was upon Amigo, still rearing and neighing, dragging the struggling grooms off their feet.

"Take me to him—at once!" the girl gasped.

Rod supported her as they half ran, half stumbled across to the frantic horse. With voice and gentle hand, Chloe soothed him and praised him and made much of him until he ceased his maddened plunging and stood, shivering, beside her.

Rod lifted her to the saddle. "Finish your performance," he ordered her. The girl flashed him an enigmatic glance, then straightened her shoulders, and gave Amigo the word to canter around the arena.

Astley's had never heard a more thunderous ovation than greeted the pair—so ill-matched in body, so evenly matched in spirit. Three times around the circle Chloe was compelled to go, acknowledging the roar of applause. Amigo seemed quite restored, making his beautiful bow toward the audience from time to time, without Chloe's needing to give him the signal. Then, finally, she guided him away toward the stables. Behind her she heard Astley's great voice bellowing that the culprit who had set the fire had been apprehended, and that they had just been privileged to witness the first leap through fire by horse and rider, which feat would undoubtedly be performed again at a later time.

"Do not forget you saw it first at Astley's!" he concluded.

At this moment, one of his grooms came running up to tell him that the roof had caught fire from the star-bursts, and that he had better advise the patrons to get out before they got hurt. This Astley was quite able to do, and so powerful was his stentorian voice, and so persuasive his performance, that the withdrawal from the building was accomplished without any injury other than twenty cases of the vapors and three fainting fits.

Meanwhile Rod, ordering the grooms to stable Amigo with an extra bait of corn, bore Chloe off in his arms to the boarding house. Janet joined them as he was carrying the girl up the stairs, and hastened ahead to open the doors and light the lamps. Rod deposited his dripping burden on the side of her bed. Then he turned to face Janet grimly.

"You will undress this woman and tend to any burns she may have acquired. And then you will go down to the kitchen and make her a cup of tea, which you will bring to me."

"And then I may get myself lost," Janet thought. A short time later, downstairs in the front hall, she ran into Lord Randal and Sir Peter, both exceedingly anxious as to the health and well-being of Miss Chloe Keith.

"She's safe in her rooms," Janet said, and the happiness of her smile assured them there was no serious injury. "Roderick is with her."

"Oh," said Lord Randal, and then, *"ah!"*

"Just so," beamed Janet.

"Will you offer Miss Keith my compliments upon the finest show of gallantry I have ever seen?" asked his lordship. "And give her my best wishes—and Mr. McLeod my congratulations! Also, when you judge it is a fit time to tell her, inform her that the man Amigo savaged, the villain who set fire to the hoop and to the oil he had poured on the water in the trough, is still alive, although badly injured. His name is Peke—but I think he will be very grateful to be allowed to absent himself from London for a while, and will certainly not prefer charges against Amigo!"

"He is wise to absent himself!" Janet said angrily.

"Just so," agreed Lord Randal. "You might also wish to tell Chloe that Astley's is in the process of burning to the ground—no fatalities, thank God, but a complete loss of the building. It was the fireworks."

"Mr. Astley *will* be pleased," said Aunt Janet happily. "Nothing Mr. Hughes could do would *ever* top that!"

The gentlemen took their leave amid a warm exchange of compliments. Janet went on into the kitchen to make the tea, debating whether she would have the courage—or the foolhardiness—to intrude upon that couple upstairs with it.

* * *

The couple upstairs were glaring at one another with emotions far different than Janet was attributing to them. Chloe's were a disturbing mixture of joy at seeing Rod again, alarm at his cold, set expression, and extreme discomfort from the ducking she had received on top of her bad cold. Oh, yes, she thought, eyeing the Laird warily, she and Lady Barbara could laugh about how easy it was for a clever woman to manipulate her man—but when one was face to face with him, big and virile and very much his *own* man, how then did one begin?

In the event, it was not she but Rod who opened fire.

"I hope you are satisfied!" snapped the man Chloe realized she loved. "Endangering your life—are you *sure* you are not burned?—and making a public scandal of yourself in the most revealing garment I have ever seen upon a woman in public!"

Chloe glanced down at the sensible nightgown which now covered her body as completely as a canvas tent would have done, and with much the same effect. Rod caught her glance.

"Not that thing, of course! Although it is hideous and quite unsuitable!"

Chloe did not ask: unsuitable for what? She hoped she knew.

Rod was going on angrily, "Do not try to defend it! I had you in my arms, remember, and am well aware of the effect a dip in water has upon that flimsy material! To think that you rode three times around the arena in a garment no more concealing than a windowpane!"

"*You* threw me on Amigo," the girl protested. "*You* told me to ride!"

"Well of course! It was the best thing for both of you, at that moment. And do not tell me you would not have made the ride had I not told you to! I have some knowledge of your courage, girl! Don't seek to gammon me!"

Chloe's predominant emotion now was anger at his continual scolding, when even a dunce would have realized that when a girl is sick, and tired, and has just been nearly drowned and burned to death in the same accident, what she wanted was not condemnation but caressing.

"Who could succeed in gammoning the great McLeod? When you always know what is best for everyone—!" Chloe was full of her own outrage that she barely heard Rod's low-voiced question.

"I know what's best for me, I think. When shall we have the banns proclaimed?"

The girl's shock of incredulous joy quite unnerved her, and she stared sharply at the man. "Banns? What sort of rig are you running now, you bad-tempered, changeable, obstinate, *perfidious* Scot?"

For he had cut the ground out from under her anger in a very devious and ungentlemanly way, she realized. How could she stay at outs with the man who had just said—had said—

A little stiffly, Rod was answering her. "As a matter of plain fact, if you are making a catalogue, I am even-tempered, rational, steadfast, open-minded and loyal."

Chloe, thunderstruck by this evidence of his complete ignorance of his own character, snapped back, *"Even-tempered!* How can you have the—the *brass* to say so to me? When upon my first meeting with you, you were arrogant and mocking and sneering, and called me a—"

"Whist, woman!" Red-faced, Rod interrupted her tirade. The even-tempered Scot was showing every sign of working himself into a fine passion. "You English never forget nor forgive, do you? You know why I acted as I did that evening. I have seldom lost command of myself in my adult life—and usually, it seems," he ended wryly, "with you."

"With that knowledge of our antagonistic personalities, I wonder you should consider such a ridiculous thing as—as calling the banns." Chloe faltered over that delightful phrase, but rallied and rattled back gamely, "You know we continue to rub each other the wrong way!"

Irresistibly Rod's lips quirked into a grin. "What a trenchant turn of phrase you have, love! I must admit that the idea of rubbing you—"

Scarlet-cheeked, the girl lifted a warning hand. "Don't *trifle* with me, Rod McLeod—!"

"Now that's another very pleasant idea! Keep talking, love, and you may finally give me the answer I wish to hear."

Chloe fumed. Give him the answer, indeed! He hadn't asked the question! And how could any self-respecting female presume he meant—whatever he did mean, and confess to more than he maybe wanted to hear, before he'd really asked her? She had not realized that love involved this painful embarrassment. Still, for something so important, she must make an effort. She drew a deep breath.

"I hadn't thought the very eloquent Laird of the McLeods would be such a slow-top in action," Chloe said, provocatively.

"You little vixen, how could I press my suit? What with Beresford and Daley and Peke and who knows how many more dangling after you, I decided you'd want the entrée to the Beau Monde one of them could offer, the revel-routs and great balls and parties—"

Chloe began to chuckle. "Can you imagine *me*—" and she held out her arms to display the huge, sensible nightgown, "at a great ball? I'd be hopelessly at sea among all the painted, bejewelled ladies and silken gentlemen. If you claim you can picture me in that scene, you are a greater fool than I thought you."

A dangerous glitter appeared in Mr. McLeod's eyes, and he was understood to say that he knew very well where he could picture her—grimy, maddening, irresistible little limmer that she was, and if she didn't mind her tongue he would join her there immediately, banns or no banns!

This terrifying threat seemed, oddly enough, to reassure the girl. "Have you—actually—spoken to the minister?" she asked, looking anywhere but at her companion.

The glitter in Rod's eyes was replaced by a dawning smile.

"I may have just hinted a bit to the good man," he said, primly, with the twinkle that disarmed her while it enraged her. "Of course, you'll ken I made no definite commitment, me not knowing whether the young lady was of the same mind as myself—"

"Oh, Rod, you great fool, I love you," cried Chloe, and held out her arms.

"A handsome declaration," said the great fool, and sitting on the side of the bed, took her into his arms.

"And you'd better," advised Chloe from the depths of that impressive embrace, "make a *definite commitment* as soon as possible, for I like this," and she gave him a hard, hot little kiss, "a great deal too much!"

Rod uttered a triumphant shout, and returned the kiss heartily.

Janet, halfway up the stairs with a tray of tea, paused, turned, and retraced her steps. Not for all the tea in China would she have invaded that room at that moment. Smiling, she returned to the kitchen and drank the whole pot of tea herself.

Chapter Seventeen

MILORD RANDAL BERESFORD returned to his home very late that evening, a prey to mixed emotions, and also, it must be admitted, to the brandy he had imbibed. Sir Peter, deciding from a hint or two which his friend had let fall that such succor was indicated, had haled Lord Randal off to his father's house and plied him with a bottle of Daley *père*'s choicest brandy, which the senior Daley had been saving to celebrate his heir's marriage. Since Lord Daley, together with Randal's father and Barbara's, was attending upon the Regent at Brighton, this rapine was not discovered until much later, when—but that is another story.

Pleasantly mellowed by his potations, his chagrin at the little chit's choice of a different protector fading into a gentle regret for the might-have-been, Lord Randal entered his home very late—or, to be accurate, very early the next morning, to be greeted by a disapproving butler.

"What the devil are you doing up, and with that Friday face, Bates?"

"There was a note brought around just after you left the house tonight—er, last evening, Your Grace," answered Bates in condemnatory tones. "It was the Lady Barbara's footman brought it, Your Grace, and he said to tell you it was urgent—*most urgent,* he was instructed to say."

"Then why the devil didn't you send him after me to Astley's, you old humbug?"

Bates frowned his disapproval of this aspersion on his dignity. "For the reason, My Lord, that I had not been informed you were going there. Perhaps if you, Sir, had taken the trouble to apprise me of your destination—!"

"Aye, you'd like to have me on rein, as though I were a child in leading strings, wouldn't you, Bates, you old humbug?" retorted Lord Randal, chuckling reprehensibly.

"You're disguised, Master Randal," said the old retainer crossly. "Now get you into the library and I'll bring you something to restore you. I have a feeling the Lady Barbara has gotten herself into some coil or other, and her father is at Brighton and not that much help even when he's here, as you know very well, Your Lordship!"

This mournful statement served to sober Randal's elevated mood. After the restorative, which left him grimacing, he nonetheless felt so much more himself as to demand to see the urgent missive. When this was put into his hands, he first sniffed at the delicate perfume which wafted from it, then grinned, "Minx!" and finally settled himself with furrowed brow to scan the contents.

Two minutes later he was out in the hall shouting for Bates.

"Coffee, to my room at once! While I'm changing into buckskins and a riding coat, get my racing curricle to the front door! Bustle, man!"

Ruefully aware that his feeling about her ladyship had been correct, Bates bustled to such good effect that Milord was able to mount his curricle, purse filled, head as clear as could be expected, within twenty minutes of the time he had first entered his house. He had decided not to take his groom, Fenn, since he felt the fewer who knew of Lady Barbara's folly, the better. As he drove at a rapid pace out of the metropolis, Lord Randal had a sudden chilling memory of another disastrous journey, several weeks back, in which Fenn had not been included, and hoped very much that the horrors of the Smoulton expedition would not be repeated.

The George and Dragon, the inn which the Lady Barbara had mentioned in her note, was a scant hour's drive north of London, but by the time he reached it Lord Randal was as angry as he had ever been in his life. He turned his curricle over to a sleepy ostler with a sharp command, "I shall be requiring this again very shortly. Tend to my cattle!" Then he strode into the hostelry.

A little to his surprise, the landlord met him in the hallway, and greeted him very civilly, considering that the dawn was just lightening the sky. Before Lord Randal could speak, his host said, "If you will come this way, sir? Miss Jones is waiting for you."

If there had been the slightest hint of a leer in the fellow's manner, Lord Randal would have dealt him a freezing set down, but the landlord was solemnly deferential, as though it were the merest commonplace for a gentleman to enter his establishment before dawn.

Grimly the Duke followed the obsequious figure up a flight of stairs and to a door near the front of the house, where he knuckled the panel softly.

"Come in," instructed a well known voice.

Grinding his teeth, Lord Randal nodded dismissal to his guide and opened the door. Confirming his worst fears, Lady Barbara, in a remarkably fetching costume, sat before a glowing fire. Of her escort there was no sign. Lord Randal addressed his childhood friend in a voice of iron.

"You will put on your cloak and accompany me back to London at once," he commanded.

Lady Barbara, pale but alert after her night-long vigil, shook her head. "I am not quite ready to leave, Randal."

"Have you taken leave of your senses?" he snapped, closing the door and advancing toward her. He took her note from his breast pocket and quoted: " 'I am meeting the man I love at the George and Dragon, one hour north of London, tonight. I hope we will soon be married. I tell you this partly because you are my oldest and dearest friend. I know you will wish me happy. B.' . . . Barbara, who is this man who has so little care for your reputation or your happiness that he would meet you in this clandestine way?"

He glared around the spacious room, saw the remains of a small meal, and noted, with inexpressible relief, that the bed had not been slept in. "Where is he? Not yet arrived?"

"He is here." Barbara's smile held a sweetness which tore at Lord Randal's heart. His eyes searched the room again.

"Under the bed?" he mocked. "A gallant cavalier indeed!" Then his voice changed, roughened. "Oh, my dear! You don't—*can't*—realize what you are doing! No man worthy of your love would put you in such hazard.

Come home with me now, and if you really want this fellow, I'll—I'll see to it somehow! But not in this hole-in-corner way. You can't want—this!"

"But it is exactly what I do want," insisted Barbara, giving him her newly radiant smile.

With one fierce movement he was beside her, had pulled her up into his arms and held her hard against his beating heart.

"No, my little love! I cannot let you go to this laggard who does not even show his face! Is he asleep next door? Where is this ardent lover?" He took a deep, steadying breath as he scanned the girl's lovely face and met the clear open gaze of her beautiful eyes raised to his. "Barbara—sweetheart—we have been blind! I cannot let you go with this man. You must marry me!"

"To save my reputation?" asked the girl. Eyes lowered, she played with a button of his riding coat.

"Yes," began the Duke, and then he put one strong hand under her chin and raised her face to his. "No, my own dear one. Not to save your reputation nor to please our parents or titillate the *Ton!* You must marry me because I have loved you since first I saw you, a little red-haired darling looking up at me so trustingly at your eighth birthday party—"

"And you fought Gervais when he wanted to whack me and he gave you a black eye," teased his lady.

"But you must admit I bloodied his nose very effectively," he protested, smiling down at her so lovingly that the girl's heart beat faster in her breast. She met his ardent glance.

"Have you really—loved me all these years?"

He bent and kissed her lips gently. "I must have done," he admitted. "I came here ready to horsewhip the man and drag you home with me."

"But I thought . . . Miss Keith?"

The Duke settled her more cozily against his strong body.

"No, my love, Chloe is a great-heart, and a charmer, but she isn't a bewitching, provocative little beauty who holds my future in her two smalls hands." He lifted them and placed a kiss within each palm. "Besides, she's marrying her wild Highlander," he added, injudiciously.

Lady Barbara stiffened and withdrew a little in his embrace. "Is that why you are turning to me?"

Lord Randal pulled her back close to him with a masterful air. "No it isn't, you little goose! I've always known you were the only girl for me. I was just waiting for you to grow up. Now come with me at once before everyone in this hostelry is awake to gape at us! I want to get you back home safely. And just to make sure we have no more such harebrained starts, madam," and he kissed her lightly on the tip of her exquisite nose, "I shall send the notice of our engagement to every newssheet in London!"

"You are very domineering, sirrah!" said the Lady Barbara, but she said it with an adoring smile as she picked up her cloak and reticule.

The man's hands were warmly possessive, draping the cloak over her shoulders and fastening it beneath her rounded chin. "One kiss, to plight our troth, my darling," whispered her lord softly.

She came eagerly into his arms, and the kiss was long and sweet. Then, very masterfully, he advised her to pull her hood over her head, escorted her down to the waiting curricle, distributed such largesse as had the host blinking and the ostler grinning, before he gave his horses the office to go.

Lord Randal Beresford drove his one true love back to London in the brightening dawn. It was not until several days later that he bethought himself of the

223

suspiciously elusive swain, and demanded to know the name, style and direction of the fellow. When his lady, smiling mischievously, told him that *he* had been the man she expected to meet—"for I knew that letter would bring you, Randal!"—he was already too besotted by his love to do more than threaten her with a hideous punishment at some unspecified future date. Then he allowed himself to be persuaded to settle for a delightful embrace and the promise that the Lady Barbara would never write such a letter again.